Amazing Offer!

An Anthology Edited by S.D. Vassallo
and Elle Turpitt

Amazing Offer!

Edited by S.D. Vassallo and Elle Turpitt.
Copy edited and proofread by M.J. Pankey.
Formatted by Stephanie Ellis.

Cover illustration and design by Ellen Avigliano.
www.imaginariumarts.com

First Edition: June 2022

ISBN (paperback): 978-1-957537-29-0
ISBN (Kindle ebook): 978-1-957537-28-3
Library of Congress Control Number: 2022938123

BRIGIDS GATE PRESS
Bucyrus, Kansas
www.brigidsgatepress.com
Printed in the United States of America

This anthology is dedicated to all the people who ever had to flee their homes.

Content warnings are provided at the end of this book.

Contents

Acknowledgements

We'd like to thank Ellen Avigliano for her enthusiastic contribution to this project. The fantastic cover she created for this anthology is sure to garner attention.

We'd also like to thank Elle Turpitt, M.J. Pankey, and Stephanie Ellis for their technical work. This project wouldn't have left the 'cutting room floor' without their expertise.

A thank you to all the authors who contributed their stories to this anthology.

A big thank you to 'the gang' from Discord: Max, Kim, Laurie, Cindy, and Steph, for their support and encouragement. You guys are awesome.

And thanks to C.J., wherever your journeys have taken you.

FOREWORD

Thank you for purchasing this book! A quick glance at the world news will alert you quickly to the humanitarian crises around the world, and the countless numbers of people fleeing their homes for a better and safer life elsewhere.

People flee their homes for a number of reasons: war, natural disasters (like the earthquake that occurred in Afghanistan just as this book went to print), religious persecution, unrest, and climate changes. This book went from idea to reality as we watched in horror as people tried to flee Syria. Since then, there have been a number of natural disasters, more famine, Russia invaded Ukraine, and there's a rising need for safe places in Central America for people in the LGBTQIA+ community.

The International Rescue Committee (IRC) does a much-needed job in helping those refugees find a new home. Their work is critical. By purchasing this book, not only have you obtained a fantastic collection of tales and poems, but you've helped the IRC with their work.

So, thank you, and enjoy the anthology!

Learn more about the IRC at: www.rescue.org

Amazing Offer!

QUIETLY, I GO

by Cindy O'Quinn

Quietly, I Go
My thoughts spread across eternity…
I sleep just long enough to jump from one nightmare to the next. The place between alive and living, where the voices of depression succeed in boring a hole into my spirit. My soul.
…mind ruminating on the day you left
There is no heaviness which can hold a candle to sorrow, unless it's regret. Maybe they are one and the same. It's anyone's bet, when harm is what they do best.
born of one lone event
Giving up the ghost is never easy—unless it is. I've given on more than one occasion. The ghost, that is. Three to be exact, but the damned thing came back.
rinse and repeat…
Back to life, back from the dead. Twice by my own volition. Once was someone else's decision. Strange as it sounds. Strange but true.
…until life takes hold
To be free of flesh and bone takes time. It's not something you can do on your own. Time, that is. Timekeeper—keeping time.
they will come and go
I hear them calling. Calling. Sounds from above or below. Tiny faces, tiny hands, and tiny teeth to show how best they love. Devour and taste the scent of youth—
woven among their blood
They come to seed the fields, row after row of flesh and bone. The ones who come to collect all souls as their own.
watch as they come and go
When my head is full of dark thoughts, I carry you close. Lingering moments catch as though haunted by your ghost.
I wear your aura as my own

Drawing invisible hearts around your memory. Make a wish, and watch as it floats away from my today, and into the arms of your tomorrow.

...initiation into darkness

Notwithstanding my fight to recover. The sound of descent, swings like a pendulum, close to my broken mind, and sets my teeth on edge.

human nature frays at the hem...

You are my prison. Possession is the warden, standing guard—taking hold. Death's coffin opens to welcome me home. Feigning hope, I let go. Now I lay me down.

Quietly, I go

A Taste of Honey

by Catherine McCarthy

A REMEDY FOR EVERY AILMENT, the sign above Driscoll's Drugstore boasted, and right there, in the middle of the window display, an arrangement of glass bottles next to a sign which read, *Hamlin's Wizard Oil: elixir for all ills.*

Mildred peered closer, the prospect of a cure for her rheumatism making her old heart flutter. It had taken her almost an hour to shuffle her way to town, and her hip was as sore as a grizzly bear. The door to the drugstore tinkled a warm welcome as she entered, summoning Driscoll the druggist from out back.

"Well, well, if it isn't Mildred Musgrave," he said. "Good to see you. And how is that old hip of yours?"

The grimace of agony on Mildred's face answered for her as she eased herself up on a stool and pummeled her right buttock with a balled fist.

"I'm at the end of my tether, Mr. Driscoll," she said. "This pain's as sharp as a knife, I tell you."

"Well now," he said, rubbing his hands in glee. "I might just have the cure." From the back shelf he produced a glass bottle and slid it across the counter with the ease of a barman in a Western. "Hamlin's Wizard Oil. Cures all ills, especially rheumatism."

While Mildred examined the bottle, he sauntered over to the window display and came back carrying the poster she'd spotted. Proud as punch, he held it up for her to read. Mildred's eyesight was sufficiently acute for her to make out the image of an old man and woman. The woman leaned in close, whispering in a conspiratorial fashion in the man's ear. Her left hand nursed a cup, and on the table stood a bottle of Wizard Oil, uncorked and ready to do battle.

Dan Driscoll stabbed the poster with a fat digit. "This here's the wizard himself," he said, pointing at the old man in the picture. "Came right on in just yesterday, swearing he'd created the cure for all ills."

Mildred screwed up her face. "Huh, sure don't look much like a wizard to me."

Driscoll the druggist was no pushover. Dan the Doubter some called him, so Mildred was astonished to see he'd fallen hook, line, and sinker for a home-made recipe, cooked up by some travelling tinker.

"You don't have to wear a pointy hat to perform magic, Mildred."

Mildred pointed to the list of ailments on the poster. "What's it supposed to cure?"

Dan Driscoll peered over his spectacles and, in a voice smooth as honey, read: "Hamlin's Wizard Oil. The greatest family recipe for rheumatism, toothache, lame back, diarrhea..." He stole a breath. "I tell you, Mildred, this flaxen liquid is the elixir of life. Made from the purest honey and propolis, straight out of Wizard Hamlin's very own hives."

Mildred's scowl suggested she wasn't convinced. "And what makes you so certain?"

Driscoll stepped from behind the counter and paused a few feet in front of Mildred before hoisting his trousers to the knees and displaying his ankles. "Look," he said, grinning like a cat that got the cream. "No swelling."

Mildred had to agree, Mr. Driscoll's varicose veins stood proud, but his ankles were as slender as bamboo stalks.

"A single teaspoon is all it took. It's a miracle, alrighty! I've tried everything over the years... Epsom salts to elevation, magnesium to massage, but none of it worked." He skipped back to his serving spot behind the counter with the zest of a seven-year-old. "Now then, what can I get you? One bottle or two?"

Mildred's husband Merle raised his eyes to the heavens as she plonked the bottle down on the table.

"What you gone and spent our hard-earned cash on now, woman? Another darned quack remedy?"

"I knew you'd say that." She puckered her lips in spite. "It's all right for you, Merle Musgrave, you don't have to put up with this darned hip."

Merle tilted the bottle to read the words etched onto the side of the glass. "Wizard Oil? You gotta be kidding!"

Mildred snatched the bottle out of his hand and flipped him across the head.

"You haven't seen what it's done for Dan Driscoll's ankles. You wouldn't be poking fun if you had. One spoonful, and not a bit of swelling in sight. Now, if you don't mind, I'm giving it a try, and perhaps you ought to do the same for that frozen shoulder of yours. You've been on about how you can hardly steer the darned tractor, perhaps this'll sort it out."

She was right, of course. Merle Musgraves' shoulder had frozen so badly these past months he could barely raise his arm more than ninety degrees. Snatching his keys from the hook, he stormed out of the kitchen, calling over his shoulder as he went, "You stick to your mumbo jumbo; I'm off to kill me some weevils, they're playing havoc with the corn."

The bottle of Wizard Oil came without dosage instructions. Mildred conjured the poster to mind, remembering the cup that sat in front of the old woman. Should she dilute it? But Dan had sworn his swollen ankles had been cured with a single teaspoon of the elixir. She'd swallow it neat, what harm could it do?

The amber syrup coated her tongue, sending her taste buds into a frenzy. Cotton-candy sweet with an undercurrent of caramel came through first, but once swallowed, the sensation of warm buttered toast, coated in brown sugar, remained behind. Most pleasing indeed, so much so she was tempted to take a second spoonful. She quickly replaced the cap to prevent herself from succumbing to temptation.

***

The following morning, Mildred woke to the serenade of the meadowlark and the sensation that all was well with the world. No pain, no stiffness, she swung her legs out of bed and stood without the help of a cane. One step, two steps, and before she knew it she'd reached the bathroom without a hint of soreness. Her heart skipped a beat at the prospect of being pain free. It had been such a long time since she had been this agile. Why, she felt thirty years younger! She couldn't wait to see Merle's reaction. This ought to shut him up.

She washed and dressed without the help of her sock-assist, before sacrificing her cane to the incinerator. Merle might say she was jumping the gun, well he could go cock his rifle elsewhere. She sat at the farmhouse table with a pot of coffee and a hunk of bread, heaped with blueberry jam, eyeing up the bottle of Wizard Oil on the sill. She would save this morning's dose till after she'd eaten, that way she could savour its sublime taste for longer.

"Well, sweet Jesus!" Merle said, watching Mildred scatter corn to the chickens with neither a cane nor a care in the world. "Maybe I ought to try me some of that darned Wizard Oil."

Mildred did a little jig. "Told you, Merle Musgrave. Waste of hard-earned cash, you said. Huh!" She licked a forefinger and struck the air.

***

By the end of the week, word had spread and Driscoll's Drugstore had completely sold out of the golden elixir. Driscoll hoped and prayed that the wizard would put in an appearance soon so he might replenish his supply.

He didn't have long to wait, for two days later the shop bell rang and in strolled Hamlin himself, complete with a large travel case and a wide grin.

"I see no sign of Hamlin's Oil in that there window display, sir," he said with a wink. "Am I right in thinking you're out of stock?"

Dan Driscoll patted his forehead with a towel, the heat of the day and relief of the salesman's arrival making him sweat. "You are indeed," he said. "My customers tell me their rheumatism, dicky tummies, asthma, you name it, are all cured... Mr. Hamlin, I do believe you've created a little miracle."

It was late August, and already the tips of the maple leaves were tinted red, the wheat grain ripe and golden, and the sugar beets ready for pulling. Hamlin placed the travel case on the counter and teased open the buckle. Thirty bottles of Wizard Oil lay in neat rows, their contents slowly settling with a satisfying glug. "I must warn you, this is all I can let you have until next year's harvest."

Driscoll's face fell.

"Before long, I'll tuck my bees in for winter and allow them to cluster. What honey remains in the hives belongs to them now. It's only fair." He saw the expression on Driscoll's face and quickly added, "But, hey... next year it'll start all over again."

***

Hardly a day went by that winter without someone begging Dan for a spare bottle of Wizard Oil. Bribery, flattery, tears, you name it, but of course he had none to give. He wished he'd had the foresight to withhold a few bottles for his more desperate customers, the genuine few who needed urgent treatment. He would plan ahead next year, he promised himself.

The more canny townsfolk, those who had purchased an extra bottle or two, sat on their precious bottles like hens on eggs.

In many ways, the scarcity of Wizard Oil began to highlight who amongst them were the most benevolent, those willing to share a little with those most in need. On the other hand, it also emphasized those less generous, the greedy few who, despite the fact they were completely well, refused to admit to possessing the golden elixir. Of course, Dan knew otherwise, but customer confidentiality prevented him from taking to the street and shouting out their names to all and sundry. Yes, next year he'd be more careful about who he sold it to.

***

As summer faded to autumn, and the days wore long shadows,

the townsfolk anticipated the wizard's appearance. A buzz of excitement grew around Driscoll's Drugstore, and the little square in front of the shop became a hive of activity. Dan was pestered so often he found it necessary to place a huge sign in the store window, promising to inform the townsfolk of the wizard's arrival the moment it happened. The sign read:

No need to get a bee in your bonnet...
When the wizard arrives, I'll blow the bugle
and you can make a bee-line for the store!

And that's precisely what he did, except this time he logged each customer's name and recorded the date whenever he sold a bottle of Wizard Oil. He'd attached his own labels too, labels which read: *Hamlin's Wizard Oil, strictly one purchase per household, per annum.* Dan made sure to hand each customer a label along with their purchase and learned to ignore the disgruntled complaints that issued forth from their lips.

***

When Ursula Wilson of Loganberry Lane wandered down to the lake and returned home with a soaking wet dress and a three-pound bass in her basket, no one batted an eyelid. At the ripe old age of seventy-five, her husband Jack had to admit Ursula's behaviour had been a bit erratic of late. If it hadn't been for the dress, he'd have thought she'd found her way to *Fishing For Compliments Seafood Store*, just like she'd intended. After questioning her about the incident he learned otherwise, though how on earth she caught the bass with her bare hands neither of them could say. She'd been taking Hamlin's Wizard Oil for arthritis and it had done miracles for her finger joints. Perhaps the answer lay therein.

However, a few days later, when her husband Jack failed to find his way home from Butler's Bar and ended up wandering the woods till dawn, both grew a little concerned. Five nights a week he'd gone for a nightcap since as far back as he could remember, and not once had he ended up anywhere other than home, no matter how much bourbon he drank. Husband and wife agreed: something inside their heads felt off; both were plagued by a buzzing sensation that made them feel disorientated.

All it took was a little poking about to discover they weren't alone. Tales of memory loss and lapses in concentration were rife among the townsfolk. And there was one thing they all had in common: each and every one of them had ingested the new batch of Hamlin's Wizard Oil.

Some folk refused to believe the golden elixir had anything to do with it, maintaining the benefits far outweighed any side-effects. A handful of folk stopped taking it, just in case, while the odd few turned up at Driscoll's Drugstore demanding a refund, insisting this year's batch of Wizard Oil was contaminated.

"When's that wizard due back?" Amelia Jackson said, slamming a half-filled bottle of oil down on the counter. "I'd like a word with him."

But poor old Dan had not the faintest idea. Wizard Hamlin had sold him the whole year's stock and was unlikely to return before autumn. Dan also refused to believe the anomalies in people's behaviour had anything to do with the oil; after all, he still swallowed a teaspoon every night before bed and it had done him no harm. His ankles remained skinny and pain-free, and apart from a bit of tinnitus, which he put down to old-age, he felt as fit as a fiddle.

Then things took a more sinister turn.

One night, shortly after helping one of the ewes birth its lambs, poor old Merle Musgrave suffered a seizure, one that caused him to thrash about like a fox in a trap before losing consciousness. The incident turned to tragedy when his wife Mildred ran to fetch help, for instead of turning right into the town square, she turned left and headed for Buffalo Springs. By the time dawn broke, Merle was dead, his tongue bitten in half and his head resting in a pool of vomit.

And that wasn't the end of it. As autumn leaves fell to the ground, one by one, so did the townsfolk.

***

Wizard Hamlin arrived in the square just in time to witness the last maple leaf tumble from the tree. This time, instead of a travel case, he pulled behind him an empty cart. A buzz of anticipation flowed through his veins when he saw how devoid of life the town was. Apart from the wind in the trees, the only sound was the gentle hum from the cloud of bees that swarmed around his head, sleepy and placid.

As they drew close to Driscoll's Drugstore, the queen bee led the parade, closely followed by her attendants. This would be her final season. Her eggs were laid; a new colony waited in the wings, and soon she would die.

She came to rest on the drugstore windowsill from where she studied the poster on display, not a bottle of Wizard Oil in sight. Then up she rose, with what little strength her wings could muster, and headed out towards Musgrave's farm.

The sheep bleated a warm welcome as they grazed the field, and the hens clucked with excitement, for they had not had company for several weeks. The air was filled with the promise of fall: ripe plums and cinnamon spices.

Hamlin's bees swarmed with excitement, a frenzied, hovering hum that he wore as a wizard's hat above his head. He knew where to find the culprit: in the barn, beside the crop-sprayer...

DDT Insect Killer, the flagons read, *Good for row crops, helps farmers pass those gains along to you.*

Hamlin kneeled on the ground with his head in his hands, while the bees settled on his shoulders. As he stood, the swarm rose with him, all bar the queen. She remained on his collar, her head bowed low and tiny tongue hanging out. Hamlin let her rest there while, one by one, he loaded the flagons of insecticide onto the cart. Then he held out the palm of his hand and the queen obliged.

As the sun dipped on the horizon, Hamlin lowered his queen to a flowering chrysanthemum, her copper abdomen camouflaged against the petals.

"Sleep well, my queen," he said. "You have done your duty and now it is time to do mine. Rest assured, your offspring will not suffer as you have done."

Her huge eyes, all-seeing, watched him leave.

"You reap what you sow, I guess," he said to no one in particular, for there was no one left to hear him.

MADAME'S WONDROUS TOILET MASK

by Sarah Jane Huntington

"Madame Rowley's Toilet mask or face glove. A natural beautifier. Soft, flexible, and can be worn without discomfort. Simply attach at night and awake to a marvelous complexion."

Estelle reads aloud and cackles with laughter over her find. The advertisement and packaging on the old box seem both ancient and absurd.

Did women really use these things? she thinks. And go to bed wearing them, ha!

She's been crawling around in her mother's dusty attic for hours, and discovering such vintage items hidden away gives her a brief and fun respite.

So far, she has set aside two large boxes and both are full. One is labeled 'Junk,' the other 'Sell.'

She wonders which box the beauty mask should go into.

Surely the curious find would have some value? After all, it must be a hundred years old or more, and the packaging looks to be in good condition too. It might be worth a try; there are people who collect all sorts of odd things.

She sneezes loudly. Dust flies up and catches the sunlight streaming through the gaps in the roof. The pretty sight makes her feel as if she has a thousand galaxies swarming around her.

For a moment, she takes a brief slice of time to mourn her mother. It feels strange to have to sort through her belongings, she had no idea she was such a hoarder.

"MUM!" calls a voice from the floor below her. "Are you done yet? I'm hungry."

Her daughter, Maxine. Age sixteen, permanently glued to her phone and seemingly unable to make a sandwich by herself.

"Almost!" she calls back.

Estelle's task is an unpleasant one. Still, she has to clean the house out and try to sell it now her mother is gone.

She plans on making a fresh start with the proceeds of the house and its treasures. God knows she needs it.

For years, she has lived only half a life.

She has been torn between caring for her mother and looking after her own family. Yet her attempts at a careful balancing act blew up in her face. Her mother died alone in her bed, without Estelle by her side, and her husband found the attention he craves in someone else's bed entirely.

Now, her future looks uncertain. Gray instead of the vivid colors she hoped she might see.

Estelle is only forty-seven, but because of her appearance, she believes she will never find anyone else.

She never has the time to take care of herself the way she cares for others. There just aren't enough hours in the day.

While her friends wallow in hot baths and visit expensive beauty salons, while her husband conducts his affair, she is running around trying to please others as always.

She is living in a state of permanent exhaustion.

"MUM! I said I'm hungry!"

Estelle groans loudly.

Her situation needs to change. She longs to have time for herself. Even a single hour in a day would be enough, to begin with at least.

When was the last time she was able to sit and read a book? She can't recall.

When was the last time she was able to enjoy a walk in the sunshine? She has no idea.

"MUM!"

An old handheld mirror catches her eye. The center is cracked in a single straight line. She picks it up, meaning to throw it in the box marked junk, but instead stares at herself.

One side of her face appears warped, and it looks as if she is two people and not one.

Truly, that is how she feels inside.

Dark shadows surround both eyes and thick wrinkles gather in the corners. Not laughter lines; she has nothing to laugh about. Tiredness and stress mark her features. Scars of being taken advantage of or walked all over are prominent.

Her hair is dull and lank, she can't remember the last time it was cut.

She sighs loudly, furious at the image glaring back at her. The reflection is of someone she never wanted to become.

***

Estelle had high hopes for a happy life. She had once dreamed of taking long holidays in the sun and working in a job she found thrilling. She still yearned for nice, designer clothing instead of the charity shop outfits she wears, and longs for passion and romance, but most of all, she longs for peace and quiet.

She has none of those things and none are in sight.

Her marriage is as tired and dull as her hair, her children are anchors that bind. She has the responsibilities of one daughter, and three boys she and her husband share custody of.

She often thinks that in life, a person needs to be spoon-shaped, smooth, and graceful, with a fine arch and the ability to hold whatever is given.

She feels more like a fork. All sharp prongs and hard edges.

Maybe I should go to a spa? Once the house is sold. I should treat myself.

Are her hopes little more than an illusion? Her children need clothes and one is off to college soon. There might be nothing left for her.

She picks up the vintage mask and frowns. Maybe she shouldn't sell it.

It's old, yes, but what harm could it do to use it? It might work.

She shoves the mask into her jeans pocket and scrambles up. She will finish up another day, she has sandwiches to make.

***

Later that evening, Estelle sits in front of the mirror in her mother's old bedroom. She is living in the house until it is sold, simply because she has nowhere else to go.

Her own former home is off-limits. Her soon-to-be ex-husband has moved his mistress in, his much younger mistress, and discarded her, the one he made vows to.

"You're old, you've let yourself go. You never have time for me." The last words he ever spoke to her. The insults are etched into the layers of her mind.

A knock sounds at the bedroom door.

"Come in," she says. It is eight at night and for the first time in a long time, she is hoping for a quiet evening. She is so tired that her bones hurt.

Maxine pops her head around the door.

"Can I have some money? I want to go out."

"I don't have any."

"Oh my God, you are *so* useless! I should live with Dad."

Estelle feels a ball of upset rise. A tsunami of pain she struggles to keep a lid on.

"Stop it," she answers. "Ask your dad for money then."

"Fine. Whatever," her daughter says and slams the door.

Tears begin to flow. It's all too much. Her mother dying alone, her marriage failing, her hopeless future, her dreams destroyed. The constant worry about money, the struggle to buy even basic food. The loneliness, the despair. Being thrown away for a younger, upgraded version and having no time for herself. She does not want to be inside her own skin anymore.

"It all needs to change," she says.

She often talks to herself; she is the only one who listens to her own words, or maybe she is talking to her deceased mother who died in the room she sits in.

I will find the money for a break, I will. I'll keep some aside for me. I'll dye my hair, I'll find a job. I'll put myself first for once. I'll buy new clothes and have a real makeover.

These are promises she makes weekly and breaks daily.

Her eyes stray to the curious old fashioned face mask.

Why is it called a toilet mask?

She shrugs and assumes it must be the first of its kind. Now, everyone uses collagen-based cloth masks or expensive chemical peels. She cannot afford either.

She picks up the packet and roughly opens it.

Surely it's long out of date?

It doesn't smell rotten or ruined, in fact the scent is quite surprising and alluring.

She feels as if she is lured, pulled, caught in the charm of what might be.

I'm meant to wear this all night? Anything is worth a try, I suppose.

She imagines she will wake up glamorous and beautiful; she pictures handsome men at her door, all wanting to whisk her off and treat her like a queen.

Her hot tears dry as she smiles at the idea. If only.

The mask has fixtures attached that wrap around the back of a person's skull. She places it over her head and slides it into position.

She can just about see through the eye slits.

She giggles, knowing she must look odd or strange, almost like a horror movie villain, the one that goes around killing frisky teenagers.

And yet, the texture feels nice. Her fraught skin feels instantly cool and calm. Perhaps the mask might heal her issues after all.

She shrugs and lies down for a nap. There is still a lot to do in the house, it's best she gets some rest while she can. Besides, inside her dreams, she can be anyone.

***

All evening and night she sleeps soundly. Even when her daughter sneaks in and takes her last five-pound note out of her hiding place in her purse, she doesn't wake.

When her phone rings at eight in the morning, she still doesn't wake, and when the post falls loudly through the letterbox, she is still sleeping.

At ten, her daughter comes into the room and pokes her.

"Get up, you missed taking the boys to school. Dad's angry."

Estelle begins to stir. She's been having wonderful dreams of old-fashioned London streets and smartly dressed individuals.

"Pardon?" she says.

"Mum, you've slept for like fourteen hours. Get up!"

Have I?

She resists the urge to sit up in a wild panic. So what she's slept for all that time, she feels wonderful.

She stretches and enjoys the rare sensation.

For once, her bones aren't hurting. She has none of the aches, stiffness, and pains that usually greet her when she wakes.

She blinks rapidly and wonders why she can't see clearly.

Oh! The mask. It's been on all night.

"Are you getting up then or what?" Maxine complains. "We've no food again."

Estelle loses her train of thought. Where is she? Everything feels peculiar. The wallpaper in the room is different, yet the same. Her body feels brand new and yet old.

"MUM!" Maxine yells.

"Where are your manners, young lady? One should speak eloquently at all times," Estelle finds herself saying.

Why did I say that?

"What?"

"Hush child, give me peace."

She feels irritated by her daughter. Surely she has taught her better manners? Perhaps she hasn't, or the lesson didn't reach her brain enough.

Well, that will absolutely have to change. She won't tolerate such uncommon speech.

She swings her legs out of bed and stands. Her posture is different, she holds herself ramrod straight.

"Where are my things?" she asks. "My corset and my dress."

"Have you gone mad?" Maxine asks.

Estelle stops, feeling strange. A curious sense of déjà vu engulfs her.

What am I saying? I don't wear corsets, do I?

It certainly feels as though she should. She has a sense that she should most definitely wear a dress, trousers would be an absolute outrage and not befitting of her status.

"Get that thing off your face, you look like a weirdo," Maxine informs her.

Oh yes, the mask. It was only meant to stay on overnight.

She sits back down on the edge of the bed and tries to think clearly. Her thoughts feel tangled. As if there is an intruder inside her brain fighting for space and pushing her away.

What feels right is not her usual idea of correct.

Perhaps I'm coming down with something?

She resists the urge to swoon and take to her bed for a week.

Her hands reach around her head to remove the mask, except, there is a problem of some magnitude. It will not come off.

"It's stuck," she tells her daughter. "Help me please."

Maxine pouts and puts her phone down. She grabs the edge of the mask and pulls slightly. No movement.

"Pull harder!" Estelle orders.

Maxine does, pulling with all her strength. All she achieves is dragging her mother off the bed until she lands in a heap on the floor.

"Is it glue?" Maxine cries. "It's like superglue! Google says you might be having a stroke too because you're acting weird."

"Fetch the doctor at once!" Estelle shouts. "I require immediate assistance and fetch my chamber pot also."

"What are you on about? Chamber what? What doctor? Doctors don't come to people's houses!"

"Of course they do, child, we're ladies, not peasants."

"What the fuck, Mum!"

"Language! That is an obscenity! Now, fetch the maid and ready the carriage."

Maxine stands with her mouth wide open. Mother and daughter

only stare at each other, each as confused as the other.

What am I saying? Am I still me?

She only wanted some peace and quiet. She only wanted to look prettier.

A sharp pain ripples inside her mind, a further invasion or attack. For her, the world feels upside down and back to front. Of course, doctors attend to ladies in their homes, except they don't.

She knows this. And nor does she have a maid or carriage. She has a car, but then again, she *feels* she must own an immaculate carriage. She *feels* a doctor should arrive and prescribe her a remedy, a tincture perhaps. She likely has a fever or caught a chill.

"I'm ringing an ambulance, you've had a stroke or something," Maxine yells.

What on earth is an ambulance?

She is in her nightclothes, it won't do to be seen by other people wearing her nightclothes, why that alone would cause a scandal and it might even make the society section of the papers.

The light switch in the room flicks on. Estelle screams at the sight. Candle flames enclosed in a glass! Why, such a thing can only be sorcery.

It's only a light switch, that's all. Not a gaslight. Remember.

Her true memories are fading rapidly. A wave of dizziness and confusion carries her away.

Gone is the pain and the scars her husband left behind, gone are her fears and worries for her future.

As Maxine flees out of the door, she stands and crosses to the wardrobe.

She is still mourning her mother, she will have to choose a black outfit before anyone arrives or she might bring shame down onto the family name. She should prepare tea and be ready to accept guests in the parlor room.

And what of the mask? She catches sight of herself in the mirror. Her hair is thick and untamed, entirely changed. She stands tall and resolute, fierce in her nobility and status.

She likes it. She is quite happy with her appearance.

"Dad," she hears her daughter say. "You need to help us, something's wrong with her. Come quick."

No. He can't come to her home, she does not want to see that wicked scoundrel with his liar's tongue.

***

Minutes later, Estelle drifts regally down the stairs. She holds her head high and prepares herself for visitors. She has found an old black dress of her mother's and a hat. She cannot find hat pins at all, which has infuriated her.

"What the hell are you doing, Estelle?"

Who is Estelle?

A vague part of her mind realizes she is the one he speaks of, or at least, she used to be.

Her ex-husband Eric stands at the foot of the stairs. He is dressed in a jumper and baggy jeans. It is, for her, an unsettling sight. She would rather be a widow than become abandoned by such a common man.

"Get out of my home or I shall summon a policeman," she tells him.

"You need a loony bin," he says. "You've lost it."

Lost what?

Estelle does not know what his words might mean. A spark of thought surfaces before it is quickly quashed and made to vanish.

"What's that on your face?" he adds.

Her mask feels as if it is part of her and perhaps now, it is. The thought of being without Madame Rowley's toilet mask is far too chilling to contemplate.

"Leave at once! You scoundrel," she hisses. "You beast, you fiend. Scallywag! Philanderer!"

"What the…" Eric gasps.

Outside, colored lights flash. For a moment she flinches, unsure and afraid of what might be out there.

A sense inside her tells her she is safe. She is a scorned woman but not one meant for a workhouse or some wretched asylum. No, not her. She is from noble birth.

Maxine opens the door.

"Please serve us tea," she tells her daughter. "I shall be in the parlor."

***

Scenes become blurry for her. Estelle tries with fierce strength to find a way back to herself. Instead, she is silenced. Drowned from the inside until almost nothing remains.

Men in uniform assess the mask stuck tight to her flesh. She is outraged by their touch.

At first, she is polite to her guests, as a lady should be.

"I'm quite happy, thank you," she repeats with great stoicism.

The strange men do not believe her.

One claims they have to take her away.

She bites and kicks and tells them that she is a lady.

She finds herself sedated and shuttled off to a cold white building.

A kind-looking gentleman in a white coat tells her things she cannot understand.

"The mask is woven and interlaced with your own skin," he says. "We cannot remove it without great risk. I've never seen anything like it, the threads run deep into tissue and nerves."

Threads run deep. Threads.

The word reminds her of embroidery. How she always loved to sew. She likes to sit by a window and gaze out across the land, needle in hand. She came to adore the peace it gave and yearns for it now.

"Tell me your name," the man says. "You appear to have suffered a disconnect from reality. Do you remember your name?"

Yes, of course, she does.

"I am Madame Rowley," she says.

What a silly man he must be, to not know the name of his own patient.

"And the year?" He asks.

"Why, nineteen hundred and one."
Gosh, he really is a fool.

***

The staff in the unit refer to her as Madame, as do other patients.

She is treated very well.

Twice a week, she gets to leave the walls and wander the gardens along with her parasol if the sun is too harsh.

If rain falls, she sits by the window and creates her embroidery flowers. She can read a book anytime she likes. Mostly, she is content within the walls she cannot leave.

The mask remains embedded on her face. No one mentions her appearance, no one mocks or challenges her.

She does not recall a time before she wore the mask. She only knows who she is now and she is resolute in her beliefs.

The world is different, yes, it is terrifying and noisy, but she remains the same.

She is the lady of a big house called a secure hospital and she is quite happy, thank you.

After all, she finally has her peace and quiet.

LINES OF BEAUTY

by Simon Clarke

Ladies,
WOMEN AND WOMEN ONLY
Are competent to appreciate
SOAP,
And to discover new uses for it daily.

Ladies,
All beautiful women
Like good wine.
It has no equal,
For all Female Ailments.

Ladies,
Disfiguring, itchy, burning, bleeding,
Scaly, pimply humors,
Vigor's Horse-Action Saddle,
A sure cure.

Ladies,
Beetham's Glycerin Cucumber
Instantly relieves,
Without leaving odors,
During the changing weather of spring.

Ladies,
With a little perseverance,
Rhine Violets, and Bovril,
Children disappear as if by magic,
Keeping the skin soft and smooth.

SIDHE & SUNKIST

by A.E. Fiori

Her father's truck smelled of dust and—faintly—of an orange grove. Packed earth, water, rot, sun warmed leaves, oranges, and the barest hint of orange blossoms. The dust made itself seen as well; motes danced through the air as they jostled over a dirt road and branches brushed the doors in welcome.

Morgan was as content as could be; her dad had to do a quick check on some equipment and, since it was Saturday, she could tag along. The second he'd mentioned the name of the grove, P32, both of the women in his life were interested.

P32 held secrets. Her mother was hopeful he might scout the tiny stand of persimmon trees tucked inside, and make sure the crop would come in well in the fall. Not that he wouldn't have, the whole thing was his responsibility, but her mother liked to make sure. Morgan was hopeful they might pass by the horse corral and see if the white horse was there. Deeper in the grove, away from the road, was a single horse corral, and sometimes there was a white horse in it. If the horse was there, she would be allowed to sit on the rails and stare as her father worked. Her mother liked to joke that the white horse had brought her since the stork couldn't.

As they rolled through the grove, she spotted the spindly branches of the persimmon trees her mother loved. "Let's stop here." Her father threw the truck into park. "The well I have to check is just a few rows down."

"Can I go look for the horse?" Morgan noticed a stack of crates piled high, each having an ad on the side. Her favorite was always the Royal Knight. There he was, tucked away behind a few other crates. Proud on his horse, armor glinting in front of hills full of orange trees. She liked to pretend her father was the knight. Her father liked to point out that the castle in the background didn't have a gate or drawbridge. No way in or out.

Her father waved her away. "Go on, and I'll find you when I'm finished." He caught her eye before she could move away. "The rules are the same as always. Don't trust anyone you don't know. I don't want to lose you out there."

Each row was wide enough to drive a truck down, but these trees hadn't been trimmed yet this year. Errant branches reached out across the empty space to shake hands with their neighbors. Morgan ducked and wove as she set off. She burst out, breathless, and heard a snort. There was the mare, snowy white and looking at her intently.

Morgan moved slowly and quietly to the fence. Then she simply stared, her eyes drinking in the mare's beauty and wishing intently she knew what it was like to have a ride. There was a movement in a tree nearby. Her gaze went to it to find two sets of eyes staring at her.

She couldn't look away. Fear started to creep in. If they were staring at her, what would they do when she looked away? Whoever they were? Her eyes started to water. A flicker of white came into her peripheral vision. The two sets of eyes blinked as the mare stamped and snorted. Muffled swearing came from the tree as two tiny men stepped out.

"Get off with ye, ye great interferin' beast!" One of them grumpily flapped his arms at the horse. She huffed and danced away. The other picked twigs and leaves from their clothes. The first slapped a red hat on his head. "And ye, what do ye think ye are looking at so hard?"

Morgan gripped hard onto the fence rail. It felt like the world spun once and then settled. "I was looking at you, in case I looked away and you disappeared."

The one with no hat picked another leaf from his partner's back. "Thought we were leprechauns, did you?"

"I didn't know what you would do if I looked away. Are you leprechauns though?" They both made faces and Morgan took that as a no. "What are your names?"

They looked at her aghast. "Imagine, us givin' our names to a changeling child just because she asked!" Red Hat was turning red in the face.

Morgan narrowed her eyes. "What did you call me?"

"A changeling child! What else would we call ye?"

"I don't know what that is." Morgan almost told them to call her by her name, but stopped. If they couldn't be polite enough to introduce themselves, she didn't have to be polite back. "Just 'child' is fine," she said.

No Hat blinked. "A changeling child does not belong to their parents," he began.

"Oh, I already know I'm adopted." Morgan shrugged him off. "Everybody knows that. It's not a secret. And I don't belong to anybody except myself, so there."

Red Hat hopped about, incandescent with rage. "No, ye great idiot! Ye belong to the fae. There's Sidhe blood in those veins of yours, ye mucking buffoon!"

Morgan didn't know what most of that meant, but she could recognize an insult anytime. "Takes one to know one," she said. She thought Red Hat was going to explode.

No Hat didn't seem to mind. "What are you here for, child?"

"I'm just here to visit the horse. What are you doing here?"

"We are here to make sure our lady's *horse* is properly cared for. But since you're here…. We've a different sort of opportunity."

Morgan felt a stab of panic. "You're not going to kidnap me, are you?" She eyed the little men. There was no way they were faster than her running through a grove.

"We cannot touch ye, Child." Red Hat spat. "A deal's a deal. But yer father, on the other hand—" They looked at each other and melted into the shadows and sunlight. Morgan gasped. Icy fear trickled down her spine. She didn't know exactly what they meant or what to do, but she had a terrible feeling in her stomach.

The mare crept closer while Morgan was frozen with fear and indecision. Breathing softly, the mare lipped her sneakers, then the hem of her jeans. When her head was level with Morgan's chest, she gently nudged her and whickered. In the sound there was a quiet voice. "Don't worry, go find your father."

Morgan ran her hand over the mare's velvet muzzle. "Thank you," she said, and leapt down from her perch. She dashed straight down the row, heading for the lane they had driven in on. Her father's truck wasn't there any longer. Her heart sped up. He said he would be near the well. She started trotting along, looking down the rows for his truck as she passed. She started to spot damp ground.

Morgan sped up. The well was down one of these rows, but where? The chain link fence and tin roof over the pump appeared without warning, including more and more puddles of water, but her father's truck was nowhere to be found. She dashed away. Was she lost? Impossible. There was no way for her to be lost in a grove.

Then, just as she was beginning to get a stitch in her side, the truck was there at the opposite end of a row. And between them was damp earth, sprouting tiny mushrooms in a rough circle.

Her father had shown her these, of course. A fairy ring, he'd called them. They say if you step in the ring, they can take you away. Don't go messing with the faeries, he'd said. She'd never seen one in the groves. Too dry. Oranges like deep drinks, not sips from puddles.

Slowly the truck jostled over the dirt lane between the trees. She waved her arms, hoping he would stop. Her dad smiled and flicked his fingers from the steering wheel in his driving wave. The wet patch of dirt spread out from the well, ringed with mushrooms. She took a step back, hand to her mouth.

The truck rolled forward, crushing the first edge of mushrooms and squelching mud over the rest. She stepped under a tree as her father stopped the truck and leaned over to pop the door open. He was grumbling. "Just look at all the water wasted. Someone's not been checking in here properly."

Morgan climbed in. "Didn't you see the mushrooms, Dad? You just drove through a fairy ring! I tried to warn you—"

"Oh, the faeries will need more than a mushroom ring to catch your old dad. They've been trying for years. Now, how about some ice cream?"

She caught sight of two sets of angry eyes disappearing into the leaves. "Sounds good."

THE MODERN WOMAN'S GUIDE TO SUCCESS

by Patricia Miller

Mrs. Virginia Barnes watched from her front porch as the last cage was loaded onto the truck, headed for who knew where. She wouldn't miss the canaries any more than she missed the frogs which preceded them. Not that she hadn't been successful, mind you. She'd made enough money breeding frogs for French restaurants to purchase a breeding pair of birds, an incubator, and cages, and enough money off the birds she was successful in raising to start her next venture. She waited on the porch long enough to meet the mailman with that afternoon's offerings, hoping the new issue of The Modern Woman's Illustrated Monthly would present a suitable business opportunity.

"Saying goodbye to all those birds, Mrs. Barnes?"

"It was time, Mr. Palmer. They were ready to spread their wings."

He laughed as she knew he would.

She collected her mail and returned inside her snug little bungalow. It was smaller than she was used to, but she'd given her former residence to her son and his bride, now expecting their third bundle of joy. She would have been happy to share the home – it was plenty big enough – but her son demurred, hemming and hawing around the reasons why they didn't want her living there, even though they were more than happy to spend money on a housekeeper and live-in nursery maid.

She accepted their decision without a fuss, just as she accepted her sudden widowhood three years before, the barely adequate pension her husband's partners at the accounting firm offered her, the friends who no longer called because widowhood might be contagious, the bungalow the children had found for her, the tedium of her daily life.

"I suppose I could become one of those women who focuses

on good works or volunteers at hospitals and soup kitchens." It sent a shudder through her zaftig frame. She was too young at fifty-one to settle into *that* kind of an existence. She wanted to be doing things. She wanted to learn things. She wanted *something*.

What that *something* was turned out to be an ad on page 68 of the current issue just delivered by Mr. Palmer:

To Modern Women Everywhere!

Did you contribute to our country's efforts during the Great War by keeping the home fires burning and offices running like well-oiled machines?

Do you miss the excitement and challenge?

Do you know your way around an adding machine?

Did Uncle Sam teach you to type?

Are you proficient in either Pitman or Gregg shorthand?

Brush off those valuable skills and run your own small business at home! Opportunities are available part- and full-time for well-motivated women who can support local businesses with secretarial and bookkeeping services.

You can create your own schedule around naptime, dinnertime, any time!

For a small investment, Barley Business Systems will set you up with our invaluable book, *The BBS Modern Woman's Guide to Success*, a customized business plan, sample ad copy for your local newspaper and, for a small monthly payment, a typewriter and adding machine you can use to build your own business and pad your own nest egg! For more information send a SASE to Barley Business Systems at the address below.

It's never too late to become a Modern Woman!

"Well, that would suit me perfectly!" Virginia read the ad aloud, momentarily forgetting there were no longer any birds in the cottage to serve as a captive audience. She *had* all those skills and, more importantly, some cash on hand. She wrote a short note expressing her interest and tucked it into the envelope along with the self-addressed and stamped envelope as requested.

***

After a short correspondence, the business plan arrived, along with *The BBS Modern Woman's Guide to Success*. Virginia studied both from cover to cover while awaiting delivery of the typewriter and adding machine. She prepared flyers and filled the built-in cupboard meant for china with paper, carbons, and envelopes. Three weeks later, Mr. Palmer delivered the heavy boxes to Virginia's door, generously carrying them to her tiny dining room, now converted into an office.

"Another business venture, Mrs. Barnes?"

"Yes, Mr. Palmer. I'm setting myself up to support small businesses in need of help. Not all of them can afford a full-time secretary or bookkeeper, you know." She primed the pump carefully, just as the book outlined. *The BBS Modern Woman's Guide to Success* had been quite clear about how valuable the mailman was, '...*for who knows the lay of the land better than he who walks it every day?*'

"That's a great idea, Mrs. Palmer. Why just this morning, Mr. Pitfield down at the garage said he was having trouble with his accounts. How about I let him know you're available?"

"That would be most kind of you, Mr. Palmer. Let me get you one of my flyers, and perhaps you can pass it along."

"Better give me several of them. If I hear of anyone else needing help, I'll send them your way."

***

And just like that, Virginia gained the Pitfield Garage account. Mr. Palmer spread the word, and she was soon working steadily.

Such a feeling of accomplishment! Not all of it was as interesting as her war work had been, but there was satisfaction gained with every deposit in her savings account at the bank. She paid off the note on the adding machine and typewriter, and while she wasn't making a fortune, it was a nice supplement to her small pension.

Virginia had enough work to keep her busy most mornings. That seemed to be enough for her needs, and she considered the possibility of refusing any new clients when she was contacted by a Mr. Richard Weber, referred by Mr. Pitfield, who serviced his car. Mr. Weber was a few years younger than her, plain to look at, an engineer who worked for the utility company.

"Doesn't the utility company have a secretarial pool, Mr. Weber?"

"It does, Mrs. Barnes, but my needs are for an independent project, a hobby if you will. I've been assured by Mr. Pitfield that you're prompt and accurate with your work. Most importantly, you're discreet. My work is highly confidential."

"I'm no gossip, Mr. Weber, and I know how to keep a secret. As long as you are doing nothing illegal, we won't have any issues."

Virginia wasn't risking her future on anything shady.

"Oh, it's nothing like that, ma'am. I'm an amateur ham operator, and I build, uh-h, model planes, but some of the message traffic and design prototypes must remain confidential." His smile transformed his plain face into something much more interesting.

Virginia tried to hide a blush. 'That shouldn't present any difficulties then, Mr. Weber.'

***

Mr. Weber was a steady customer, unlike many who only needed her services for billing cycles or end of the month correspondence. Sometimes he just handed her notes to transcribe, printed in that precise engineering penmanship. Since she could not travel to his place of business to take dictation, he was often found on her front porch when weather permitted, and in her dining room/office when it didn't. He would sit in her late husband's armchair, and she would sit at the dining room table, pen at the ready. He was the easiest of her clients, her favorite client, if she was being honest, and his work was just so interesting.

She didn't know a great deal of the terminology he used, but Mr. Weber took care to spell out the more technical words. After a few repetitions she had no difficulty spelling propulsion systems, extrusions, aerodynamics, deceleration, elliptical dihedral… She didn't know what any of them meant, but she could spell them correctly and that was all that mattered.

Her son didn't approve of her working. He approved even less of Mr. Weber. "He's making himself right at home here, Mother, and the situation lends itself to unseemly gossip."

Virginia glared at her son over the rim of her reading glasses. "I have done nothing wrong, certainly nothing to cause gossip."

"You don't need to be *doing* anything to be gossiped about. Appearances matter and this is just the sort of thing Lillian and I fret over."

Virginia took a deep breath, counted to ten. She was *not* going to engage in an argument about her son's wife. Lillian registered her first complaint about her mother-in-law five minutes after the wedding when she let her new husband know that Virginia's elegant blue mother of the groom attire wasn't appropriate for a woman her age. Their relationship had gone downhill from there. Elliot Jr. loved Lillian, and Virginia learned to pick and choose her battles, mainly by retreating as often as she could.

But this was not a retreat she was willing to make. For one thing, she had done nothing to warrant such gossip (if indeed there was any — she would not put it past Lillian to make the whole thing up). For another, she appreciated having the financial independence the Barley Business Systems made possible. And for a third thing, she liked Mr. Weber, although the less said about that to her son, the better.

"Elliot, I appreciate the concern you and Lillian have for my reputation, but as I said, I've done nothing wrong, and the extra income has been a godsend." She paused, then went in for the kill.

"I *suppose* if I didn't have to worry about utilities and bills for the bungalow, it would be easy to turn away from my little business…" She gave him an innocent look (*The BBS Modern Woman's Guide to Success* had an entire chapter outlining ways to deal with disapproving family and friends). She knew he wouldn't return home and tell his wife his mother was moving in.

He backed down just as the guide said he would. "Fine. I suppose it's not anyone's business. After all, you're old enough to be past that kind of thing anyway."

Oh, how she bit her tongue. She was *not* too old if her dreams were anything to go by. And she *did* have dreams, lovely dreams about Mr. Weber and his wonderful planes, and the possibilities of where they might go. But perhaps Mr. Weber thought her old. She took a long hard look in the mirror after her son's departure. Her hair was a nice shade of brown, barely any gray at all, and Elliot Sr. had always claimed her full figure made her a nice armful. Maybe a new dress or two wouldn't go amiss, but she was what she was, a woman in her fifties, perhaps too old for romance, but not yet past wishing for it.

***

Mr. Weber's visits increased throughout early spring and the letters became more technical in nature. She struggled with the complex subject matter, even though she had gone to the library and checked out a book on aviation principles. She wasn't sure why a plane would need a launch rail, or what a Newton-second was. And the radio traffic made even less sense. Much of it wasn't even in English.

Mr. Weber was quick to point out that ham operators used codes, much like the military did, and he assured her the odd combination of numbers, symbols, and letters made sense to his counterpart at the other end of the transmission. He was very strict about the messages, double- and triple-checking them for accuracy, so she took her time with them. There was a spate of letters dealing with something called the 'pendulum rocket theory' and another on payload – she understood the individual words, but the context escaped her completely. She didn't bother asking for explanations, but she was curious.

***

It was early May, just after lunch, when Mr. Weber came by – not a common occurrence at that time of day. She was deep into the books for the bakery when his knock jolted her back from the price of confectioner's sugar.

"Why Mr. Weber, what an unexpected pleasure. Please come in!" Only a lifetime of discipline prevented her from lifting a hand to pat her hair into place.

"I mustn't stay, Mrs. Barnes. Just wanted you to know I'll be out of town for the next week or two." He was troubled, it was plain, but she decided not to pry. Too much, anyway.

"Taking a long-deserved vacation? You've worked hard enough to earn one."

He gave her another face-changing smile. "More of a working vacation than a real one, I'm afraid. But I *will* be back." He was emphatic about that.

"Then I will look forward to your return and continuing your work. It really is fascinating, even if I don't understand any of it."

"I'm glad I found you, Mrs. Barnes. None of this would have been possible without you." Mr. Weber reached out and took her hand, clasped it in his. He bent forward but straightened back up quickly, let go of her hand. "I *will* be back."

He moved swiftly to his car, threw a speaking glance over the roof, then climbed in and drove away.

***

Life was awfully flat without Mr. Weber. She kept busy with her other clients but found their concerns about flour or engine coolant to be mundane compared to gyroscopes and wind shear. One week became two, then three. Perhaps he'd found someone else to transcribe his bizarre messages, someone with a better education, a better understanding of the science behind model planes. She hoped not, but Memorial Day came and went. There was no one she could ask about Mr. Weber. He had no family in town that she knew of, and any attempt to reach him at the utility company would only create the gossip Lillian had already tried to spread months earlier.

***

It was five weeks to the day before she saw him again. He was standing on her front porch waiting while she walked up from the bus stop at the corner.

"Why Mr. Weber, welcome home!" Oh, she was so relieved to see him.

"Thank you, Mrs. Barnes. It's good to be back. I hope I didn't worry you." He relieved her of the bag of groceries she was juggling while she retrieved her house key from her purse.

"I *was* worried. Just a bit, mind you."

He followed her through the house and set the bag on the kitchen counter.

"You weren't waiting long, were you? May I offer you a glass of lemonade?"

"That would be lovely, thank you."

"Take a seat out on the porch glider. I won't be a moment unloading the groceries and will bring it out."

She hurried through putting away the perishables, poured out two glasses of lemonade, grabbed a tin of crackers, and headed for the front porch. She paused at the screen door, watching the engineer sitting so casually on her old glider. He looked at home there, pushing with his foot to move it to-and-fro. Taking care not to jostle the glasses resting on the cracker tin, she elbowed the screen door open. He leapt to his feet and grabbed both glasses, which were teetering precariously. He waited for her to take a seat on the glider, then joined her there.

They sipped at the tart liquid, chilled just enough to frost the glasses. The slight breeze carried the smell of freshly mowed grass and early blooming roses. It should have been perfect, Virginia thought, but the man sitting next to her had a look about him that indicated he'd missed regular meals and a lot of sleep. His eyes were bloodshot, and it was obvious he hadn't seen a barber during his absence. He was also fidgeting. His left leg was bouncing, and he was rolling the glass, slippery with condensation, between his palms.

"Is everything all right, Mr. Weber? Has something gone wrong with your model plane?"

"Mrs. Barnes, would it be – that is – please call me Richard. If you like." He wasn't looking at her, but somewhere far beyond the house across the street, possibly far beyond the city limits.

"Only if you call me Virginia." She couldn't hide the blush this time. She didn't try.

"I've been calling you Virginia for a very long time. When I think of you. Which is often!"

They shared a smile across their glasses, and the moment lasted for a long, long time, but he finally broke the hold his eyes had on her.

"Virginia, I don't know how to say this. It wasn't that I intended to hide things from you, or that I didn't trust you. Please believe that."

Dear God, she prayed silently, please, please don't let there be a Mrs. Weber somewhere. "Are you married, Richard?"

"No! No, I would never – it isn't like that at all!" So indignant. She should have known better, for he was an old-fashioned type of man, with old-fashioned manners. A gentleman through and through.

She blew out a sigh of relief. "Well then, I guess anything else you have to say can't be so bad."

"Bad enough. Virginia, I won't be staying, not here."

"Not – not staying? You mean you're going away? For good?"

"Forever. I won't be returning. Not in this lifetime, anyway."

"I'm not sure what that means."

"I'm – it isn't a plane I've been building. It's a rocket."

"A rocket! Like H. G. Wells or Jules Verne?" She should have been reading her late husband's books rather than that silly volume on aviation principles.

"Yes. It was an accident."

"I don't understand how anyone can accidentally build a rocket, Richard. Surely it was obvious early on it wasn't a plane."

"It was the radio signals, you see. I thought I was exchanging plans with a fellow enthusiast. It turns out the signal came from farther away than Australia."

"What's farther away than Australia? The Russians?"

"It wasn't the Russians. It wasn't even from Earth!"

"Well, where else could it possibly be from?"

"Somewhere just beyond Epsilon Eridani."

"That isn't helpful information, Richard."

"Probably not. Let's just say it's pretty far away. But my rocket can travel there, no doubt about it. And I've been invited by the Mistra Assembly to go there, to explore the dozens, the hundreds, of planets I'll find among their member civilizations."

Virginia was speechless. *The BBS Modern Woman's Guide to Success* didn't cover rocket ships or potential suitors flying off in them. And she had thought, just minutes ago, that Richard might be considered a suitor. "And you want to go, don't you?"

"Yes."

"I see." What was there to say? Well, the guide did cover the importance of honesty, so she responded as honestly as she could. "I shall miss you very much, Richard. I have valued our - our friendship."

He stood, paced about the small porch while she sipped at the lemonade, tepid now in the heat of a June afternoon. He grabbed hold of the porch railing. The world around them was oddly silent. Finally, he spoke.

"Virginia, I have no right to ask, no expectation of an answer that will make me anything but regretful, but do you think, would you consider joining me?"

"Joining you? You mean, going in your rocket – with you?" Oh dear, oh dear, oh dear. Yes! She wanted to scream. Yes! She wanted to shout it loud enough for Elliot and Lillian to hear all the way across town as they sat in *her* parlor, ate off *her* china, while the nursery maid and housekeeper took care of all the piddly details the couple found so distasteful about living.

She tried to gather her thoughts. Mr. Weber gripped the railing tighter and tighter until the knuckles of his hands were white under the strain. He didn't press her for an answer, although she could tell he wanted to. She had come to know him well over the months they'd worked together. He wanted her to say yes. *She* wanted to say yes.

She closed her eyes, weighed out the pros and cons of such a monumental decision. She would be leaving everything she knew behind, and he said it would be forever. She would never again see her son (who had nothing to say except to offer Lillian's opinion about things). She would never again see Lillian (which wasn't a great loss) or her grandchildren (who she wasn't permitted to even take to the park without the nursery maid in tow).

Virginia wondered what *The BBS Modern Woman's Guide to Success* had to offer in such a situation. And there was the answer she'd been seeking. The next to last chapter, *Overcoming Self-Doubt*, clearly stated that most people fail because of their own doubts and fears. '*…it is wont of courage, not lack of resources, that doom many a Modern Woman. Be Brave! Take that next step!* **Make it Your Success!**'

There it was in big, bold letters. Virginia stood up, moved to his side, reached over and gently rested her left hand on top of his right one. She would make it her success. She would make it *their* success – together.

"When do we leave?"

MORE DOCTORS SMOKE CAMELS

by Allen Ashley

More doctors smoke camels –
follow the science.
They roll the wiry-haired skin
into imperfect cylinders, tamp
down the ends with a dislocated
hoof and, excuse the pun,
sit back, relax and never get the hump.
We allow their indulgences:
we need our medics onboard
in the post-apocalypse.
The abandoned zoos have proven plentiful
for fresh game, exotic pets
and taxidermy practice.
The sailors and anglers
are smoking kippers, haddock, salmon –
although what they catch
is often skinny,
unrecognizable, barely piscine.
We need our jack tars and fishing folk onboard.
The seas are rising. And rising.

DARK CORNERS

by Edward Barnfield

There is a poster in the officers' mess, hung by some wag a lifetime ago. It shows an advertisement, the type they place in railway stations; carefully peeled and shipped, then framed like some old master.

"Pears' Soap," it says. "The first step towards lightening the white man's burden is through teaching the virtues of cleanliness."

Staff Sergeant Harris finds himself looking at the poster more these days, his eyes drawn to it during the late-night drinking sessions and early morning roll calls. The joke, initially, lay in the immaculate white uniform and clipped moustache of the central figure, a world away from the sunburn and sour breath that surrounds them in Bloemfontein.

The 'humour' is magnified by the irony of its position here, in the most populous city in the Orange Free State, in the heart of Africa, where their primary role is to guard Boer women and children, herded into a concentration camp that stretches out towards the horizon. The white man's burden compounded by the need to look after other whites. Not that his comrades in arms see their charges as fully human.

"36 in the bag this week," yells Staff Sergeant Caine, elated as always. "88 wounded, 156 captured."

Caine updates the scoreboard on the wall, faithfully recording the results as though it were all a sporting shoot or game of cricket. He's of that type, you see, where his character never evolved beyond the prep school playing field.

"How many chickens?" asks Bluegrave, the camp's medical officer.

"Too many to count," laughs Caine.

Harris wonders if their enthusiasm is a product of their frustration with their current duties. Caine would doubtless prefer to be out in the veld, chasing glory and bandits across the scrub, while Bluegrave regularly complains that he's trained for field medicine, rather than for acting as camp nursemaid. Like retired sportsmen, they'd like to be adding to the total rather than merely tallying it.

Although Caine and Bluegrave did not create the scorched earth policy that they celebrate. It was established by General The 1st Baron Kitchener of Khartoum, who is moving to flush out the guerrillas in systematic drives, recording the number killed as weekly 'bags'. It is Kitchener who demands the army burns half the countryside to rid it of the farms and livestock that provide sustenance to the enemy. Each blaze creates new refugees, new half-starved families to cram into the tents behind the wire.

"Pears' Soap is a potent factor in brightening the dark corners of the earth," reads the poster.

For Harris, the number of fighters killed each week bothers him less than the number of souls squeezed into the camp. He is working with the quartermaster to try to understand how long the current rations will last, dividing and subdividing the dwindling supplies of beans, rice, and bully beef by each head. Salt beef, salt pork, preserved soup, flour, and cheese – he finds himself totaling their combined weight in his sleep, hoping to discover some flaw in the calculations that would ward off starvation a week longer.

The arithmetic has come to haunt him. Supply lines are badly disrupted, so they are working on the assumption that no new necessities will come without a significant military breakthrough. Of course, such a breakthrough would create more women and child refugees, more Black African internees for the lower camps. The scales continue to tilt in the wrong direction.

A two-tier rationing policy has brought some relief, with the families of the men still fighting labelled 'undesirables' and provided with the least. Their children look like the dead already, skin and bone and quiet little sobs, but it leaves enough for the others.

"You seem gloomy, Harris. Missing the London fog?" says Bluegrave. He is a lifer in His Majesty's forces, so of course his greatest pleasure comes from his fellow officers' misery.

"I'm worried about the camp, Bluegrave. Seems to be an awful lot of sickness. Can't you do something?"

He smiles at that. "Honestly, Staff Sergeant. I can no more magic up medicine than you could spit out black beans. These people come to us neglected and raggedy. Hardly a surprise that they fall sick."

"No sympathy for the losing side," says Caine. "Worse it is for them, the more likely their husbands are to surrender."

There is a patch of land at the back of the camp being used for makeshift funeral pyres. The smoke has been drifting upland for weeks.

"Yes, but there are cases of measles. Surely we could do more to stop it from spreading?"

"Honestly, Harris, I had no idea you had a medical background," sneers Bluegrave. "We are seeing typhoid fever, dysentery and measles in every other tent already. Probably something worse down the line. Those with a strong constitution will survive right enough. As for the rest, you should welcome a reduction in the number of mouths to feed."

They all know of Harris' obsession with the mathematics of malnourishment. He keeps a little notebook where he charts the average daily caloric intake, and they joke about his tragic tabulations.

"Attention."

The men scramble to their feet. Regimental Sergeant Major Barker is in the room, gimlet-eyed and graceless, flanked by two scowling flunkies.

"At ease, men. Now, I have a job for Bluegrave and Harris today. Challenging job. Requires a bit of finesse. Bit of discretion."

"Sir, yes sir."

"We have a visitor, at the request of the British High Commissioner, no less. A woman from England who is going to write a report on the grace and favour we are providing for our guests in Bloemfontein Camp. Lord Kitchener himself has ordered us to escort this person, to ensure that she has unmolested access to our facilities. Do you understand?"

"Sir, yes sir."

"Now, it is very important this lady goes back to England and reports that she received our support during her visit. At the same time, I want her to understand that these people are under the kind and beneficent protection of the British Empire. That we are providing a higher standard of care than what these rebels have ever received in their own homes. That we are hugging these children to our breast and suckling them as though they were our own. Can you ensure she leaves with that impression?"

"Sir, yes sir."

"Keep her on the main strand, Bluegrave. Away from the medical tent, the Black camps, and for God's sake, away from the bonfires. Tell her it's for her own good. The typhoid."

"Of course," says Bluegrave, rubbing his chin with pleasure at this new distraction.

"Harris. Show her your most optimistic calculations if you please. Food for weeks, I want her to say. Finest cooking on the dark continent."

"Sir," says Harris, hating every syllable. "Yes sir."

"Sir, can I volunteer to help, sir?" Caine jumps forward, eager as the dawn.

"For God's sake," says Barker with a grimace. "It's a woman, not a rugby scrum. Stay out of the way."

A few hours later, Bluegrave and Harris wait by the railway tracks. The day is hot, the sun merciless.

"I will wager a shilling piece that Ms Hobhouse is a dragon of the old school, a battleship in petticoats," says Bluegrave, fanning himself with a handkerchief. "Any friend of the High Commissioner is certain to frighten the horses. She will be sixty and stern, if I make my guess."

Harris says nothing. Try as he might, he cannot imagine what people back home think of this war. He knows there was excitement at the beginning as rumors of diamond mines and gold deposits filtered back, with the subsequent khaki election delivering success for the politicians. Still, as he watches the sun shimmer on the plain beyond the tracks and smells the endless smoke, he cannot imagine all this suffering would be palatable if they knew the truth. They must not know, he tells himself.

His discomfort only grows with the arrival of Emily Hobhouse. She is a slight woman, much younger than Bluegrave's prediction, but severe, unsmiling. She does not accept his outstretched hand, seems impatient with Bluegrave's oleaginous welcome.

"Can we get on?" she asks. She tells them she has already visited the camps along the coast, is aware of the mechanics of these operations. When Harris takes her to the first tent, he finds the shame almost unbearable.

"Six children, a servant girl and the mother in this space?" she asks. "And this deal box, this is the only furniture?"

"I think you'll find it's better than they're used to, Ms Hobhouse. Indeed, bringing them here is an act of the highest humanity," says Bluegrave, indignant at her attitude.

She waves a hand over the bedding, sending a swarm of flies buzzing. "Such heat under a thin canvas, Mr. Bluegrave? And these children, have they been fed recently?"

Harris finds himself viewing the refugee family through the outsider's eyes, feels the horror swelling in his stomach. A girl, the youngest, is stretched out on the bed, her limbs no thicker than sapling branches. At night, her sisters sleep beside her shrunken frame, and her mother lays on the floor with no mattress, listens to their wretched breathing. He cannot conceive of the inhumanity.

"We provide rations over and above those prescribed by law," says Bluegrave. "Staff Sergeant Harris can show you the figures. Most of the children come to us in a wretched state. The Boer women, you see, have no maternal instinct."

The mother, the woman, is in the tent with them. She shoots a glare of purest hate.

After that, each step across the camp feels like the march to purgatory. Bluegrave continues to boast, to preen, but Hobhouse drives a knife deeper with every question. She talks to the nurses, who wilt onto their beds when she interrupts their momentum. There are thirty plus typhoid patients in one tent, and a run of dysentery survivors in another, the stink and the bluebottles unbearable. The kind and beneficent protection of the British Empire.

At last, Emily Hobhouse ends the torture. She requests a brief interview with Harris, away from the internees, and strongly suggests that Bluegrave return to his medical duties. She has documented everything she has seen on this visit, unsparing commentary scribbled into a small bound notebook.

"Staff Sergeant Harris," she says. "I have to ask you; do you believe you have provisions enough to sustain the lives of the internees?"

Not knowing where else to take her, Harris is sitting at a trestle table in the officers' mess, the space empty, the two of them alone aside from a Black porter serving tea.

"I think," he shows her his notebook, a mirror twin of her own, "if we manage our store appropriately, we will be able to provide sufficient nutrition for the majority. Hopefully, supply lines will be restored soon, and we can-"

"These numbers don't tell me the story, Staff Sergeant. Is the actual quantity dispensed equivalent to the numbers prescribed in these calculations? Are the meagre rations I have seen anything more than precursors of famine?"

He thinks back to his restless nights, the numbers weighing on him like rockfall.

"And furthermore, Staff Sergeant, this is only their food allowance. What of other necessities? What of soap?"

Over her shoulder, he can see the Pears' Soap poster, can imagine the central figure turning and casting irrevocable judgement upon him, those thin lips pursed beneath the clipped moustache.

"Under army regulations, we classify soap as a luxury, madam," he says, schoolboy self-pity quivering in his voice.

"A luxury? Children in the heat of Africa, dysentery running underfoot, flies on every surface, and you consider soap a luxury?" Her face is set in stone now. "Ignorance. Crass male ignorance, helpless and muddling. Do you know how many innocents you've condemned, Mr. Harris? Can you imagine what the toll will be when winter comes?"

At that, a dam breaks within Harris, the doubts of the last few months rushing loose. He admits it, the scale of this blunder, his own incapacity to reduce its impact, to help even one of the starving children. He tells her of the volume of people poised to come to them, the dizzying number of deaths already recorded in the Black camps. He begs this stranger, this visitor, for a modicum of absolution.

And strangely, she seems to soften. "There, there, Mr Harris," she says. "I'm sure you've done your best. There are higher powers at work."

The weeks that follow are not comfortable ones. Whispers from Whitehall indicate that Emily Hobhouse's report will be unfavorable, and Bluegrave works hard to pre-emptively shift the blame onto his colleagues. Regimental Sergeant Major Barker makes it clear that he will willingly, happily transfer any and all of them to the front where the fighting is thickest, with a recommendation they be assigned to the most dangerous duties, if high command is unhappy. "We'll be adding you to the bag," jokes Caine.

Still, when he goes to sleep at night, Staff Sergeant Harris feels a strange sense of relief, of lightness, as though by telling the truth he has lifted the pressure of unmet needs from his chest. He notices that soap is reclassified as a necessity in the next round of regimental orders, in deference to Ms Hobhouse's feedback.

When the supply lines are restored, the first box that arrives is labelled 'Pears'. It is a lightening soap designed for the darkest corners.

THE GLOWING BEAUTY

by N S Ford

Have you ever spent a night in a haunted house?

I have, countless times. I'm a haunted house junkie. Whenever I hear of one, I have to check it out. I've stayed in so-called haunted houses up and down the country, plus haunted hotels, old hospitals, even a boat. To my disappointment, I never saw a single ghost.

Until last night.

This house was not the usual kind. From the outside it looked pleasant, inviting even. The garden was neat, with tidy rose bushes and a neat gravel path. It didn't stand out from its neighbours on the quiet, affluent street. I contemplated the house while sitting in my car, waiting for the owner to arrive. The building was at least eighty years old, I estimated, noting the weathered brickwork and the narrow gate posts. In terms of haunted houses, this one was young.

A woman in a quilted coat cautiously approached my window. She held up a bunch of keys between a finger and thumb, as if they were contaminated. We made eye contact and I smiled. She didn't smile back. I grabbed my rucksack and got out of the car.

"Kerry?" she ventured.

"That's me," I said cheerfully. "Nice to meet you, Mrs. Parker." I held out my hand. She hesitated, then took it. I thought she was perhaps as old as the house. Her fingers felt fragile beneath mine. Then she took a step back and appraised me.

"Well," she said. "Are you sure about this, Kerry? It really is haunted."

"I'm pleased to hear it," I responded. "How long have you owned the house?"

"Twenty years. Nobody told me it was haunted until after I bought it, if you can believe that! No one had lived there for a long time, not since the original owner died. I have rented it out occasionally, but no one stays for more than a week. It's perfectly pleasant during the day, but at night there is a glowing figure, quite terrifying. Even the neighbours have seen it, through the curtains."

"I don't scare easily," I said. That's what I say to everyone, and it's true.

She dropped the keys into my palm. "I live with my friend at number 12, at the other end of the road. You can call by tomorrow morning."

"Sure," I hoisted my rucksack. "Anything else I should know?"

"I try to maintain the house as best I can in the circumstances, but it may be a little dusty inside. I hope you understand."

"Of course," I said. "Thank you, Mrs. Parker. I'll see you in the morning."

I lifted the latch of the gate, closed it behind me, and waved to her. She nodded and turned away, plainly eager to put distance between herself and the house. It was already approaching dusk.

I tried each of the keys until I found one that fit the front door. Excited, I stood in the entrance hall and breathed in the slightly musty smell that all unaired houses have. Then I went exploring.

The house was nicely decorated, if in need of a few minor repairs. It was a pity that Mrs. Parker couldn't live here or rent it out long-term. There were three bedrooms, a kitchen, a large dining room, a separate lounge, two bathrooms, and even an outbuilding at the back with what could have been a coal cellar. An ideal home for a family. The kind of home I'd want, if I had a family. I don't even have a permanent address at that moment, dividing my nights between cheap hotels, friends' sofas and, of course, haunted buildings.

Daylight was fading. I tried the light switches but the electricity was off. That didn't worry me; I'd been in creepier places than this without it. Anyhow, it was more authentic to spend a night in a haunted house in darkness. I had a hand-held flashlight in my rucksack, plus one that fastened to my head, and I could always use my phone as a torch too.

There was no furniture at all, except for an upright piano in the lounge. The rich brown wood of the piano was scratched and stained. I lifted the lid and pressed a note, which sounded muffled and tinny. The instrument probably hadn't been tuned in decades. I laid out my sleeping bag on the floor, ate a granola bar, and went to the bathroom, where I found that the water had been turned off too.

"Hello, ghost!" I called. "I'm here! My name is Kerry. Do you want to talk?"

Nothing happened, of course. It was too early to get into the sleeping bag, so I wandered the house again, swinging the flashlight beam over the walls and ceiling.

There was a square hatch I hadn't noticed before, right in the middle of the ceiling. An attic, just begging to be explored. The hatch was small and I was big, but I was used to wriggling into tight spaces in buildings, so I knew I'd be all right. The question was how to get up there.

A few minutes later, I brought up the step ladder I'd found in the outbuilding. It was somewhat rusty and missing a couple of rungs but it seemed sturdy enough when I put my weight on it. The house was very dark by now, so I wore my head torch. Carefully, I climbed the ladder and balanced on the top step. I pushed against the hatch. It yielded and a puff of dust blew into my face. After a coughing fit, I slid the hatch to one side. I reached up and felt the sides of the square opening, hoping the attic floor was safe enough to stand upon. Then I hauled myself through, scraping my hips in the process. Perched on the edge with my legs dangling down, I wrinkled my nose at the stale air.

I pulled my phone from my combat trouser pocket. Combined with the light from my head torch, it illuminated the dark corners of the attic. At first, I was disappointed. There was nothing here, just a thick layer of dust. I twisted my body around to see the space from all angles.

That's when I saw it. A wooden chest of some kind. It had been shoved into the darkest corner, as if intended to be forgotten. Intrigued, I took tentative steps across the floor, which creaked ominously. I pulled the chest towards the edge of the hatch. I tried to open it, but it was locked, although I couldn't see anywhere to put a key in.

I dragged it out and let it fall through the hatch. Sounds destructive, I know, but it wouldn't matter if whatever was inside broke, it was so obviously abandoned and maybe pre-dated Mrs Parker's ownership of the house.

A heavy thunk reverberated from below. The chest had split open and lay in two halves.

'Yes!' I whooped. My feet found the top step of the ladder and I climbed down to examine the treasure, or trash, whatever it was.

There was a lot of stuff in that chest and it looked old, maybe a hundred years old. Letters, books, and some items wrapped in tissue paper. A stack of monochrome photographs, all of the same woman. I held the torch beam closer to the picture. She looked like one of those actresses from the Hollywood Golden Age. Immaculate waved platinum hair, snowy skin, dramatic eyes, dazzling smile, brows drawn on delicately. Her shoulders were swathed in a fur stole. The caption at the bottom of the photo said: 'Miss Cassandra Lamonta, Actress and Singer.' There was a looping signature across one corner.

"Hi, Cassandra," I said, softly. "You're beautiful." I wondered whether she'd been famous in her day. What was a stack of her signed photographs doing in Mrs. Parker's attic? I took the one I was holding with me downstairs and put it in my rucksack.

It was properly night time now. I could look through the rest of the stuff in the morning. I took off my shoes and tucked myself into the sleeping bag, switched off the torch, and put my phone down. All was quiet. I kept my eyes open, pretending I could see shapes lurking in the shadows, but this night would be the same as that in any haunted house. I'd fall asleep eventually and wake up groggily in daylight, having had a few hours of dreamless peace. And that's almost what happened.

Suddenly, I was awake, my eyes adjusting to the brightness in the room.

It wasn't daylight.

My heart pounding, I slowly sat upright in the sleeping bag. Gripping the fabric with sweaty palms, I squinted at the source of the light.

A figure at the piano, glowing bright white-green.

I quickly pulled out my phone and snapped a picture. Then I fished my sunglasses out so I could look at the ghost without searing my vision.

Her back was towards me and her piano playing was soundless. I could see the platinum hair, curled and set, her shoulder blades sharp in the backless ballgown. Hardly believing what was happening, thinking it must be a dream, I slipped out of the sleeping bag and crept closer. She made no sign that she knew I was there. I inched around to get a better view of her face.

My breath caught.

No longer the beauty in the photograph. A deformed jaw, jutting out terribly. The jaw opened and closed with an effort for her silent song, revealing gaps where teeth used to be. Lesions covered her face and neck, while her hairline was patchy. What had seemed from a distance a fashionably pronounced bone structure was plainly the skeleton rising to the surface. Eyes rolled in hollow sockets. Weakly, she finished her song, attempted a curtsey and collapsed on the carpet. The ballgown fanned out around her wasted body. As I darted towards her, she seemed to sink into the floor and vanish.

The white-green glow had gone.

I stood shivering in the suddenly dark room.

I'd always wanted to see a ghost, but I hadn't envisioned one like this, desperately sad and not at all spooky.

Peering out of the window, I saw the first hint of dawn on the horizon. I checked the time on my phone and decided it wasn't worth trying to go back to sleep. The photo I'd taken hadn't even worked properly. All I had was a black screen.

As soon as there was enough daylight, I went back upstairs to examine the contents of the wooden chest. There were concert programs and theatre bills from more than a century ago, all starring 'Miss Cassandra Lamonta'. Some letters in old-fashioned handwriting that I couldn't read much of. I came to the bundles wrapped up in tissue paper. Weighing one of them in my hand, I wondered what it could be. Finally, I satisfied my curiosity.

A vanity bag, made of black velvet with a tarnished clasp. I opened it and tipped out a jumble of little jars and pots which clinked as they rolled on to the floorboards. Some were made of metal, others were glass. I picked one up.

'Radium Beauty Cream,' the label said. 'For a healthy glow and smooth skin.'

I dropped it and examined another.

'Radium Hair Tonic – radiant, shiny locks guaranteed!'

The rest were all the same. Radium Vitamin Pills, Radium Tooth Powder, Radium Nail Polish, Radium Hand Lotion, Radium Perfume, even some kind of radium-infused belt to wear under the clothes to enhance health. Poor Cassandra believed the advertising. She couldn't get enough of the stuff and in the end it consumed her.

It occurred to me I shouldn't be handling these things. They were probably radioactive still. I swept everything back into the box and resolved to tell Mrs. Parker what I'd found.

As I took one last look around the house, my eyes rested on the piano Cassandra had played with her last remaining strength.

I wondered if her bones glow in her grave.

COFFEE BLACKER THAN DEATH

by Norbert Góra

The grains as black
as a bloody night,
is it coffee or a plaque?
It gives me such a fright.
Those eyes like mirrors of hell
reflect sufferings and evil,
words with the power of spell,
whispered by the devil's coeval.
Delicacy of flavor
or rather tar from the abyss?
Compare this savor
to a poisonous kiss.
Coffee blacker than death,
the darkest ad,
one sip guarantees a funeral wreath,
anything else to add?

SPECIAL DELIVERY

by Julie Sevens

The clattering *kathunk* against an upstairs window, and the sound like a potato sack rolling down the shingled eaves that soon followed, barely registered in Annalee's mind. *Just another raccoon*, she told herself, calming the prickle at the back of her neck. She smoothed a wrinkle in the tablecloth, the last preparation for the fancy dinner she'd planned. Her mother's wedding china spread across the table; steaming hot with mashed potatoes, piled high with rolls, arranged just so for an Insta post.

Elliot's car door slammed shut in the driveway, announcing his arrival. Annalee lit the fresh candles waiting in their holders. She put her hands on the back of the chair, waiting, decided that was too formal and swung them to her sides.

"Wow!" Elliot's bag sank to the floor, covering the creak of a floorboard upstairs. "It smells amazing in here. When you told me not to eat on the way home from the station, I thought you were getting takeout!"

She kissed him hard on the lips. His eyes settled on the table, and she could tell from the nervous quiver of his eyebrow that he didn't know what the occasion was.

"It's the one-year anniversary of when we bought the house!"

He hugged her again, relieved. "This is really amazing. I can't wait to eat." He squeezed her hands in his. "Let me just run up and put on a shirt that doesn't stink like the firehouse, okay? Five seconds."

Annalee scrolled through her playlists on Loudio, looking for just the right soundtrack.

Elliot's footsteps on the stairs became a scramble on the creaky old floors in the hall.

"You okay, hon? Did you drop something?"

Her question went unanswered.

"Elliot?" She called from the base of the stairs. Still no answer, except the crinkle of packaging. Like someone unwrapping something from a bakery.

"Elliot?" Halfway up the stairs now. A current of electricity through the air, a panicked rustling of fabric. Still no answer.

She reached the top of the stairs and heard gasping noises punctuating the silence—sharp breaths drawn as if Elliot was struggling to keep his head above water.

He was on the floor of the bedroom, his back to her, surrounded by shredded red ribbon and torn cellophane wrapping. His broad shoulders jerked up and down as he bobbed his face down toward his lap, gulping in air. Annalee's toes crunched the packaging as she stepped forward.

A loud scream pierced the air.

The first scream of a newborn entering the world, clearing its lungs, announcing its presence. Elliot turned to her, cradling the infant he'd just saved. It was a girl. The pink was just coming back to the baby's cheeks as she cried, her fingers and lips still a grim shade of blue.

Annalee grabbed the blanket from the bed and draped it over them, tucking it under the baby. She hadn't been in the room for anyone's birth—hoped never to be, she had enough child-rearing at work—and she wasn't confident what to do next. She could handle a call about a baby alone in a car at the Super Saver, or a report from a neighbor about a mom who just didn't seem to be able to take care of a newborn—she'd had two cases assigned to her like that this week—but not this. Not in her own bedroom.

Elliot stared at her, the adrenaline fog starting to wear off. "What… where'd you get a baby?"

"Elliot, I didn't."

"And why was it wrapped up in cellophane! She couldn't breathe. Oh God, Annalee."

They both looked at the baby, whose cries were softening as Elliot's arm rocked her. Elliot's breathing calmed along with the baby.

"I guess we should call 911, make sure she's healthy. Then..." She trailed off. What happens then? Who would believe this? She wouldn't believe this if it was her case.

The curtains flapped in the chill breeze, the gauzy fabric skating across the floor under an open window.

***

Annalee had spent a lot of time making her office at social services a welcoming place for families. Seasonal throw pillows, posters in a variety of languages nobody in the whole town of Chesterfield spoke, warm muted colors. She sat at a low coffee table when speaking to clients, rather than separating herself across a desk.

But today…

Today none of the things she'd arranged were familiar. She felt like she'd been plopped into a dollhouse full of chaos.

Jackie, her classmate from high school, sat across from her, holding a little bundle of blue blankets. The bundle squirmed with a tiny kick. She'd been waiting in the parking lot for Annalee to get to work.

"How have you been, Jackie? This must be your new baby! It's so nice to meet him. Tell me his name again."

"Annalee, I—this is going to sound crazy." She brushed the back of her finger down the sleeping baby's cheek.

"You can tell me, Jackie. I'm here to help." Annalee tried to remember whether the postpartum pamphlets were in the second or third drawer of her desk.

"This baby isn't Graham. He's at home with my husband. This one… He just sort of showed up."

Hand on the drawer pull, Annalee stopped. The broken window, the cellophane, the shredded ribbon. The blue-tinged baby Elliot did CPR on. The sleepless night riding in the ambulance with the newborn, finding a placement for it, leaving no time yet to stop and think about what had happened.

"This baby appeared in your house?"

"In the upstairs bathroom. Kind of like someone leaving a baby on the doorstep in fairy tales but… Well. He was wrapped in like, saran wrap, I guess. I was so worried, nearly had a heart attack to find a baby like that. But he cried when we unwrapped him." Jackie started slow, her words gaining steam like a stone rolling downhill. "I grabbed some of Graham's clothes he'd just grown out of, a blanket. I fed him a couple formula samples I had left over. And then I brought him here."

She chewed her lip, refusing to make eye contact.

"Jackie. I believe you. I—" Annalee stopped. "You're not the first person this has happened to, actually." She patted the woman's arm and watched a single tear slide from her lashes.

"We can't… I don't know why someone tried to give us a baby, Annalee. But me and Trav, we can't afford another baby right now. It's hard enough with daycare costs as it is. I feel just awful to give him to you but…" The tears flowed free now.

"It's okay, Jackie. It's okay. You're doing the right thing." She held her arms out. "Can I take him?"

Jackie clung to the baby as she handed him over, her arms unwilling to give him up.

"Jackie, we need to get him to the doctor, have him checked out. Does that sound okay?"

She nodded, her arms finally relaxing.

"I can call you later, give you an update if you want?"

She nodded again, shoulders shaking, then ran out of the office, her purse slamming against the door frame on her way out.

"Hey, little guy. It's alright, we'll get you somewhere safe, okay?" Annalee cooed at the baby. He rubbed his tiny fist against his mouth, hungry again.

***

Word spread fast in a small town like Chesterfield. Five babies in two days—full-term, healthy newborns—had been left wrapped in cellophane and a red bow inside people's houses. And nobody had any idea where they came from.

Annalee drove her car down a side street behind the diner, a five-hour-energy shot in hand. The house numbers climbed higher as she approached the sixth case. She was running out of foster placements, even with the Wallaces and the Phams both taking two of the babies. A sick feeling had developed in her gut and gnawed even harder as she tried to figure out what they'd do next.

At the house on the corner, two men in flannel shirts were nailing plywood over the second-story windows, like people on the news before a hurricane. Annalee furrowed her brow at the sky, a bright autumn blue. Down the street, workers unloaded window security bars from a van. A man in blue coveralls was already screwing in a new storm door on the porch, curls of iron protecting everything but the mailbox.

Their next-door neighbor, though, had thrown open the upstairs windows and removed the screens, despite the chill in the air. *Maybe they'll want to foster*, Annalee noted.

Number 2801 on the left now, she parked and took a deep breath.

Inside, those same shards of cellophane littered the floor of the guest bedroom. Those same shreds of red ribbon. The scene she'd walked into in her own bedroom with Elliot all over again.

This time, though, a teenage girl was sitting on the bed, tear-stained and shaking. Annalee sat down next to her.

"Hi, I'm Annalee. I'm with Chester County social services. Do you think it would be alright if we talked a little bit?"

The girl didn't move her eyes away from the broken window. "Yeah, okay. I'm Em."

"Nice to meet you, Em. Looks like you're having a rough evening, huh?"

A half smile. "I'm just supposed to be babysitting. Ryan, he's asleep. Or he was, I think the cops are talking to him now. But he's fine. His parents are on their way home."

"Wow, so you really got more than you bargained for!"

"I was supposed to go to a party tonight. I should have. But then I guess someone else'd be sitting here." New tears flowed.

"But at least I wouldn't have seen that… that thing."

"Em, you did a great job tonight. The baby—you probably saved it."

Her eyes finally peeled away from the window. "That *thing* though. The giant fucking bird. What was that?"

Annalee's heart skipped. As far as she knew, nobody had seen how the babies were appearing. "You can tell me about it."

One of the officers standing near the window straightened his back, eavesdropping. News to him, too.

"I'm not on drugs or anything. I'm a good babysitter."

Annalee put a reassuring hand on Em's arm. "I know. Actually, this happened at my house too. The first one. We just didn't see how the baby got through the window, and I'd really love it if you could help me out with that part."

"You got one too? How many people has this even happened to?" Em blew her hair away from her face. "Well, I was downstairs, and I heard this noise. I thought Ryan fell out of bed or something, so I came upstairs. I cracked open his door and he was in bed, still asleep. But when I turned around, this… well, it was a giant white bird. Biggest bird I've ever seen, that's for sure. It shattered the window with its beak and stepped in. Taller than me, it had to duck. It had a big, long neck and long legs like a flamingo. And its eyes— these horrible bloodshot eyes. It put the baby down and flew away."

"That sounds scary, Em. Thanks for telling me about it."

A little pajama-clad boy in the doorway whimpered. Em rushed over to him and clutched him up. "Let's go wait downstairs, Ryan. Your parents will be back soon, okay?"

***

The voicemail light on the greasy old phone was flashing when she sat down at her desk the next day. Mrs. Pham, asking her to call right away about the babies. Annalee chugged the dregs of her coffee from the thermos to wash down some ibuprofen and picked up the phone. Five minutes later, she was on her way back out to the parking lot.

The crowd outside the city services building had proliferated along with the plywood and bars over windows across town. *BABIES ARE A BLESSING*, one of the signs said in blue and pink block letters. *YOU CAN'T BLOCK OUT GOD'S PLAN*, read the next in black poster paint.

Mrs. Phipps, her 6th grade English teacher, stood in a blue knit sweater yelling into a megaphone about how the city had no right to have animal control attempt to catch the stork and stop the miracles. A line of animal services vans from neighboring counties was parked along the curb, and the woman kept pointing at it. Annalee was glad they didn't know about the ornithologist camped out in the mayor's office.

I wonder if they'll come in and apply to be foster parents, Annalee muttered to herself after she made it through the barrage and got in her car.

The Phams' house sat at the edge of town, under a huge oak tree. Mrs. Pham was one of their most reliable foster parents. Her wide front porch was littered with toys, her walls papered in drawings and scotch tape.

She waited for Annalee on a porch swing, a well-used travel cot next to her. As Annalee's shoes clicked on the painted floorboards, a shock of curly white-blond hair popped up above the edge of the travel cot. The baby reached out toward her. Soon, another joined—dark streaks of jet black hair above a smiling face. He gave her a grubby little wave.

"Hi, Mrs. Pham!" Annalee sang. "Are you watching these two today?"

Mrs. Pham looked at the two toddlers with weary eyes.

"That's what I called you about." Her voice was flat, missing its usual brightness. "These are *your* two. The newborns."

Mrs. Pham lifted the blond one and set him on the porch. He crawled over to Annalee and pulled on her pant leg. A bird sang from a branch in the old oak, and he pointed at it, delighted.

Annalee was afraid to make eye contact with Mrs. Pham. When she finally did, she knew this was not a sick joke.

"There's more. They've started climbing out of their cribs. We've baby-proofed the whole room, we've put a gate on the door. But they sit together in the middle of the room, in the dark, whispering." Mrs. Pham gestured to the room upstairs. She lowered her voice, as though the babies could understand her. "I hear them on the baby monitor. It sounds like whole conversations, but I can't understand them."

Annalee looked up at the nursery window. A long white feather was stuck on the sill, flapping in the breeze.

***

"Babe, pass me the napkins?"

Annalee dabbed the napkin Elliot handed her across the top of her pizza, the red-tinged grease soaking in and turning the paper transparent.

Elliot and Annalee had barely seen each other all week. They sat in the dark in front of old episodes on Food Network, shoving pizza in their mouths. Their sweatpants-clad legs were tangled together on the couch.

Elliot sighed, a deep release of exhaustion.

Once the pizza was gone, and the TV checked on them to see if they were still watching, he turned to her. "So. How was your week?"

"I can barely believe it's only Thursday." She wanted a beer, but Elliot might get called in. Annalee couldn't figure out how to tell him about the aging babies, or the feather stuck to the Phams' window. "You?"

"Nothing you didn't see yourself, I guess. Lots of 911 calls about the babies. Sightings of the stork."

"Someone actually used the Safe Haven box at the station, huh? I didn't think anyone would actually surrender a baby in a library drop-box. But… I guess none of us saw this coming. They called me to the hospital for that one."

"Yeah." His face tightened.

"You know who it was."

"Yeah. Didn't you say old Mrs. Phipps was protesting outside your work every day? Guess she didn't like it much when the miracle happened to her."

Annalee laughed. It was a hearty laugh, a decision to laugh instead of cry or rage.

"What an asshole."

They sat for a few quiet minutes when they'd stopped laughing, waiting for the other to suggest going to bed.

Elliot's phone buzzed on the side table, rattling the glass. He hesitated before picking it up and checking the message.

"Be careful, Elliot. The babies… it seems like something else is going on."

"They found the bird. I gotta go help." He patted her knee. "You always worry too much, Leelee. Just a big dumb bird."

As he was putting his shoes on, Annalee's phone went off, too.

***

The sickly lights of the hospital led Annalee down the hall to pediatrics.

"Hey, Jen. I got your call."

Her favorite nurse turned around. Her eyes were red rimmed, watercolor smears of mascara trailing down her cheeks. "You just missed the sheriff; he went with security to see the tapes. The babies, Annalee. The stork ones. They're all missing."

"Missing? Who took them?"

"I don't know, Annalee, I'm so sorry. They were in the nursery. We had seven of them here—one new, I was about to call you— and they're just gone."

Annalee sat down, trying to process. All kinds of villains went through her head, people who would kidnap seven babies from a hospital.

"Jen, can I ask you something? Did they seem… did the babies seem weird at all? Like did they seem to grow up too fast?"

Jen paused, the tears threatening to flow again. "I thought I was going crazy, Annalee. I mean this is all crazy, of course. But they did. Their weight, their reflexes; by the time they were here a day they seemed like they were a couple months old. The peds just told me, you know, we don't really know how old they were." She lowered her voice. "But Annalee, I've had hundreds of babies on this ward. They were newborns when they got here. A few days later they were rolling over, sitting up. One of them started getting her first tooth."

The sheriff sauntered back down the hallway, interrupting her.

"Jen. You run a good, tight ship here. We all know it." He leaned over the counter. "You're not going to like this, I don't think."

Annalee moved beside Jen and held her hand. The sheriff nodded to her.

"The babies, they uh. Nobody took them. They left."

"They left?" Annalee and Jen asked, in unison.

"Ladies, I wouldn't believe it either. But I just watched that tape three times. They all left. Crawled right out those doors right there." He pointed down the hallway.

Annalee's stomach dropped. "I gotta go. Sorry, Jen."

She started dialing her foster parents as she rushed out of the hospital. The ones who answered all told her the same thing: the babies were missing, the police were on the way but it had been awhile, and none of them knew what to do. They wanted answers from her, but she had none.

She drove the streets, crawling along, looking under parked cars and bushes; she remembered being in the passenger seat with her dad looking for her lost cat, Cookie, the same way. It was desperate and ridiculous, but what else could she do?

The flashing lights on Pine Street lit up the sky like red and blue lightning. One of the Animal Control vans sat in the middle of the street, surrounded by three counties' worth of law enforcement. She left her car in the road, door open.

The van's interior lights were on, and the enormous bird silhouetted the rear window. It was calm; waiting, staring. An enormous pink and red bloodshot eye pressed to the glass, unblinking. Annalee shivered at the thought it had been in her house.

Elliot found her in the crowd. He pulled her to the stone wall of a pristine flower bed across the street, at the edge of the commotion.

"That thing is dangerous."

"Elliot, the babies are missing."

"I know, half the police have been called away. But this bird, when you look into its eye—"

"It doesn't feel like any 'miracle bringer'," Annalee added for him.

Behind Elliot, the decorative tallgrass in the garden rustled. A baby giggled, stomping on the flowers.

"There you are!" Annalee exclaimed. Elliot turned around.

But the baby picked up a rock and chucked it directly at Elliot's head. It left a mark, a rising welt with a bleeding scrape in the middle. He raised his fingers to the welt, disbelieving.

"Elliot! Get over here!" one of his colleagues screamed at him. Elliot disappeared into the chaos, answering the call.

More babies crawled and toddled toward them. They held sticks, rocks, toys. Some of the gathered first responders rushed to pick them up, thrilled to see the missing babies. They were rewarded with violence; the babies smacked them in the head with their sticks, hit them with rocks, bit their outstretched arms.

The babies circled the van holding the stork. Their chubby little fingers tried to find purchase in the seals around the doors, and when that failed, they piled on top of each other and began rocking the van back and forth. The babies' frustrated squeals grew deafening.

Elliot and some of the others moved forward, tentative. Nobody had experience detaining deranged babies. They weren't willing to hurt them, couldn't bring themselves to. Could a pack of babies tip over a van? Annalee figured it was more of a waiting game—wait for them to tucker themselves out, scoop them up while they slept.

The van rocked back and forth, the tires leaving the ground. Each time they caught air, they got higher and higher, until finally the van teetered on one set of tires, then tipped over onto its side. They cooed with delight. The baby closest to Annalee plopped down and clapped his hands, thrilled at the van's toppling.

The rear door fell open and the stork climbed out. It stood tall, taller than Elliot, taller than the tipped-over wreckage of the van that had confined it. It shook its head back and forth and spread its wings wide. The babies clambered on its legs, admiring it, toddlers greeting their mom at daycare pickup.

Eyes glowing a fiery red, the stork released its staccato rat-a-tat-tat call into the air. The babies stopped, still, and turned back to the gathered chaos of first responders. Their wide round eyes lit with the same red fire, burning with fury, and they started walking—effortless on chubby legs, competent now at a skill they hadn't learned yet.

"Take the shot!" someone yelled.

One of the officers raised her gun, aiming at the bird's chest. A baby lunged at her, jumping from the ground, on her in a flash. The gun was knocked from her hands, picked up by one of the other tots, who brandished it at them.

Annalee searched the crowd for Elliot, but she couldn't see him. Her heart hammered in her throat.

The loud crack of a shotgun echoed, and the stork's wings retreated over a blooming patch of blood on its chest. It fell, bouncing on the cement, the fire draining from its eyes. The babies wailed and cried, inconsolable.

They wriggled on the ground, their limbs useless rubbery appendages again. Their newborn reflexes reduced them to jerking and mewling as their clothes grew big on them, no longer stretched over bodies that grew too fast.

Annalee recognized the baby that had first appeared in her bedroom, a pink bow in her hair matching her pink terry sleeper. She calmed for a second, looking at Annalee with alert, squinched up eyes.

Then the babies were silent, the crackle of police radios filling the air.

Brightly colored cotton onesies, patterned sleepers, and zip-up footie pajamas sank flat against the ground. Empty little hats with bears and raccoons, flower headbands, and itty bitty socks lay where they'd fallen, tiny displays of dirty and ripped baby clothes strewn across Pine Street.

The babies were gone.

REPLENISH

by Nikki R. Leigh

Like all good pyramid schemes, it sounds too good to be true. Your friend, who you haven't seen in person for over three years, appears suddenly on your doorstep, bag of cosmetics in hand, swearing her life on some kind of make-up. An all-in-one anti-aging, anti-acne, barely-notice-it's-there miracle cream.

"Apply it once a day, every day. Results immediately!" your friend squeaks out excitedly.

"How much?" you ask.

"That's the best part! The cost is so low per bottle. Makes it easy to keep up with the routine and never run out." She winks. It's as if she knows your weakness. That you've spent more time staring at your wrinkly, old face in the mirror than you care to admit. That you've pounded your fist into the countertop, again and again as the years have passed, and your face, your success, your *legacy* succumbed to the aging process.

"You have the make-up on now?" you ask, studying your friend's face.

"I do! Every day, without fail. It's not make-up, though. We call it more of a see-through face. Adding color, vibrancy, *life*." The last word drips from her lips, plump and young.

You contemplate her face, noting that it did, in fact, look silky smooth, dynamic almost, lowlights and highlights in all the right places in the most effortless way. Natural, beautiful. *Young.*

She sees your careful consideration, continues her spiel. "With this cream, you can keep your face on forever." You can't help but to feel a bit of a sinister undertone in her words, a quiet plea in her voice.

"When in Rome, or something like that," you reply, smiling kindly after a thoughtful moment. You remember seeing on social media something about your friend's divorce and lost job. You figure you can kill a couple of birds with a single wad of cash, doing a kind thing for a sort-of friend and maybe make your own life a little better in the process.

She thanks you, urging you to call if you need new stock once the bottle runs out. Promises that you'll see results within an hour and never look another year older.

You walk inside, smiling at your purchase. At this point in your life, pyramid scheme or not, you'd give almost anything a try.

***

The next morning you study your face in the bathroom mirror. A pale complexion, marred by sun and oil and lines from—God forbid—too much smiling looks back at you. Two eyes, bags underneath, dart around, taking in every mark, line, and discoloring the reflection has to offer. You've long grown weary of watching your face age by the minute, watching divots appear as if by magic overnight, certain there'd been some monster in the dark scratching scars into your skin. But no, there'd been no monsters, just the passage of time.

Like the call of a siren, the idea of reversing a downward slope into looking your age was tantalizing. You know all the platitudes about beauty being on the inside, looking "respectable" not "old," and feeling guilted into accepting and owning your physical wisdom and experience, worn on your face.

But wouldn't it just be *nice*…

Nice to look good and not just good for your age.

You investigate the bottle of cream. The label is sparse, no list of ingredients or name. Just a simple "Apply once per day, every day, consistently" written in black letters around the bottom of the bottle.

The design choice, lack of marketing, and snazzy colors takes you aback for a moment. You almost set the bottle down. Instead, you steal one last look at your wrinkled, worn face, mumble a quick, "Screw it," and open the lid. You submerge the tips of your fingers in its thick contents.

The cream goes on like frosting under a knife. It's instantly cool to the touch, providing the snappy feeling of exfoliation without the abrasiveness. You become mesmerized as you swirl the buttery cream over your face, in the crease of your nose, between your eyebrows, taking careful time in the corners of your eyes where the crow's feet have landed.

Beautiful. You look beautiful.

Just like you did on your daily news segments, at the peak of your stardom. Just like you did during the height of your pregnancy, glowing skin radiating the beauty growing within. Just like you did at your second wedding, before your daughter graduated, left for school. Just like you did when you had it all.

You nearly weep at the results. In moments, your face looks nothing like it once had, back a few minutes ago when you had nothing but a bottle full of hope. You are no longer the ex-newscaster, doomed to only write the notes, aged in your wisdom. You are no longer the mother, face worn with worry lines, wondering if your child is surviving at school, flashing those white teeth you envy so, blushing with a smooth face at partners and friends.

You're just you. All you are. The prettiest of faces once again.

***

The instructions are simple. Apply each day. Every day. And you have obeyed—the results commented on by passersby, stopping because they recognize you, they think, but from some time ago and they just can't quite place it. It felt incredible to be recognized for you, your face, the most important part of you shining on the outside.

But today—today you decided to start the summer differently. You want deeply to neglect your morning routine, no matter how short it is. So, you do.

All day, you lounge on the couch, your face clear of products for the first time in a month. And it feels great. Until—

Your face itches. It shouldn't. It is completely naked and free. But, somehow, it feels heavier than ever.

You scratch your face, lightly, but that doesn't stop the chunk of skin from detaching from your cheek, the mass of it filling your nail with a slimy weight. The blood flows from your face, the gouge deep.

"Jesus Christ!" you yell, hopping up and heading towards the bathroom. In the mirror, you take in not only the rugged valley you've carved into your skin, but the cracked mosaic of your face. You can hardly believe it's your own that looks back to you, your skin puckered and torn like a ragged piece of Styrofoam dipped in glue.

Your hands go to the medicine cabinet, past the bandages and disinfectant, and straight for your bottle of cream, which you open and smooth over your face, the thick liquid mingling with blood. Almost instantly, the cracks in your face seal themselves and the throbbing pain lessens.

You don't miss a day of application for the next month.

***

By the time two months have passed, you're nearly out of the cream.

You frantically try to find your friend from whom you purchased the product on social media, but she has vanished. You don't have her number. You search her name on the Internet, hoping to find her, track her down and demand a refreshed stock. Her name in the search bar, you hit enter, and nearly gasp at the results. Local news entries describing a grisly scene. A woman, a victim of some kind of acid attack, dead in her home in her bathroom. No suspects, just the death of another beautiful young woman at the hands of some psychopathic intruder.

You know better. She was peddling cursed wares. Her need to feel beautiful outweighed everything else, so she traded her life to a jar full of cream. You know what she did, because now you're stuck in it too.

In just a few days, your own face will melt, slough to the floor, no beauty in death or dignity in your life.

You run to the bathroom, pull the jar from the cabinet. You pour over the label, willing words to appear that simply aren't there. No matter how hard you stare, there is still no product name, no way to replenish your supply.

You weep.

You sob so loud you barely hear your phone ringing over your despair. You jump to your feet, run back to the kitchen where your phone has lit itself up, an unknown number plastered across the screen.

You answer.

The voice on the other end talks slowly, clearly. "We have what you need. You'll find one bottle on your doorstep."

You try to stay calm, but the shaking in your voice betrays you. "And if I need more? How can I reach you?"

"For every person you sell to, we'll give you another three month's supply. Sell this bottle, two more will take its place. One for you, and one for the next set of months."

"And if I don't?" you ask, but you know the answer.

"You'll die as you lived, shallow, broken, and old."

"Damn you," is all you can muster before hanging up the phone.

You walk to your door, open it, and try not to jump in surprise at the arrival of the fresh jar of cream, sitting on your doormat like a bar of gold ready for the taking. You snatch it up, hold it close to your chest.

The hammering of your heart wounds you inside, each beat reminding you that you are now a predator, and you have to find your prey. You don't want to subject someone else to a life of endless vulnerability, but you also don't want to die.

You want to stay beautiful. You remind yourself it's all you have left.

Running down the list of people you could pawn the scheme to, you realize how few people you know, and how even the ones you do don't deserve this, what you'd bring to them.

Old co-anchors? Just as vain as you, but practically inaccessible. The few that quit the business had families, had made something of themselves once the camera turned off. You couldn't bear to bring that burden into another circle of people who had done more with their lives than you had managed under the same circumstances.

And family of your own...

Your daughter is too young, too pretty to have need for the cream just yet. And even if she did, her life is full of happiness and love. You're certain at the end of the day, she'd be fine with a face aged by time, knowing that each wrinkle represented the best times of her life.

And your mother, well, she is already doomed to a life of loss of self. Resting in a chair, spending a majority of the day on her back on a nursing room bed, no recollection of herself or you. Her mind is just as wrinkled as her face. You think to yourself that maybe that's the solution. Make yourself forget the rest, don't even stop to recognize the pain of dying.

You chide yourself for even thinking family was an option. You really are as ugly all the way through.

Your decision made, you go back to the bathroom, bottle in hand. Untwisting the cap, you pour. Not into your palms, but into the toilet, flushing immediately. You watch it swirl, around and around, the miracle cream hypnotizing you into thinking you made the wrong decision.

You know you didn't. You finally feel the worm of something in your gut. The feeling of doing something you can finally be proud of, that felt uniquely *you*, filling you up.

You'll take that triumph, knowing the pain will come soon. You won't say goodbye. Your family only knows the empty you and it will be easier on them this way.

On the last day of your supply, you drink, miserably, alone on your couch, wondering what will become of your face. What it will feel like despite your best efforts to numb it all away.

The next morning, you learn.

You awake with an itch that turns into a fire. You dare not look in the mirror at what feels like thousands of red ants biting your face. You know there are no insects, only the sharp stings of your face eating itself alive.

Your hands go to your eye sockets, then pull downwards over your cheeks. The flesh comes off in chunks, leaving behind a sticky, red mess.

Your forehead sloughs off on its own, draping down what is left of the bottom half of your face. Finally, your chin falls into your lap.

As you prod the muscles of your face, melting away under your touch, you curse the planned obsolescence of the cream.

Faceless, but finally ageless, you slump.

To a Lady [Somewhat Skeptical]

by Marilyn Cavicchia

You are coffee.
The very air you breathe,
which we control,
fresher than the Old South
years ago, the very hour
it was roasted.

Thursday evening: "Captain Henry's Maxwell House Show Boat"

Air is the destroyer.
It becomes stale—
quickly, completely.

Find a Friend to Eat Your Pain

by Sarah Budd

Jen had been lonely ever since her best friend, Alison, went traveling after their time together at university. Alison had such an adventure, she never came back. Last thing Jen heard was that Alison was living in the south of France with her latest boyfriend.

Jen had no one in her life. But now there was Poppy, all because Rob had allowed Jen to go out in the evening. In the meantime, he would review her receipts.

It was best she would be out of the house when he discovered she had bought mascara two days ago. Even though she had made the excessive expenditure back after purchasing reduced pork.

As they discussed the book in David's front room, a homage to all the shades of magnolia, Jen's mind wandered from the conversation. The other members of David's book club were content to sit and watch David talk and talk with blank faces. They were all as bland as the books in his bookshelves. They were just happy to be out of the house. Jen didn't just want to be out of the house, she wanted an escape.

Could Poppy become her new best friend? Gazing upon this new woman made her feel lonely, even though she had Rob and Bea. *You should be grateful,* she chided herself. Her coffee went cold. They would have so much in common, and if they didn't, Jen would just lie until they found enough common ground.

Poppy's toned figure was visible even under her thick jumper. Her spine upright and elongated in the way that only came with years of stretching. Her posture was perfect. She gave out hope. Jen reasoned that if she did yoga whilst Beatrix was taking her nap instead of watching television she could look just like Poppy. Hopefully, she would get a chance to talk to her tonight when David brought out wine and nibbles.

When eventually she caught Poppy's eye, heat flushed to Jen's cheeks, but she didn't dare look away in case Poppy thought her cold and standoffish, like all her other failed friendships. Poppy winked and grinned, miming a yawn.

David, who should have been a schoolteacher instead of an accountant, knew something was going on between them. Even if he hadn't caught their shared glances, he fathomed they were more interested in each other than the book they were here to discuss.

He brought Jen into the conversation as if she were a child being forced to converse with a grown up.

"What did you like about the book, Jen?" He frowned deeply in a way only an old man was capable of, gathering in his brows a lifetime of annoyance.

Jen was new to the book club and hadn't been fully broken in. A lot of people spouted copious amounts of rhetoric they hoped sounded right in the ears of others, copying phrases they had read straight from the Guardian or the Observer. They made her feel very stupid.

Each week there was a competition. All competing to sound intellectual and cultured. David won every time.

Jen had hated the book, she had missed its meaning. She preferred thrillers, anything with excitement. Books didn't seem to have plots these days. It was, in her opinion, a book written by a posh person for posh readers, but of course she couldn't say that. These were her people now.

"I loved the complexity of their relationship," she mumbled as she reached for a biscuit she didn't want, not now she had a new goal of attaining a figure like Poppy. "So many things left unsaid." Jen tried to hide even more in the jumper she wore to hide her mum-tum and hips that had never gone back in after Bea's birth.

The rest of the group nodded, waiting for more input, but Jen was already taking note of the warm tones in Poppy's hair and wondered if she should ask Rob to have highlights in hers. It looked so natural. She could ask Poppy what hairdressers she used. That could be a way in, something they could have to talk about until she found something that was more meaningful. Maybe Poppy had a dog. They could go for walks together.

"I didn't get it, gave up by chapter five." Poppy jumped in the discussion and made an awkward face. Everyone laughed, all relieved they no longer had to pretend.

All apart from David. "Well then, Poppy, maybe you should choose the next book."

Poppy sat up and brought out a book from her bag. "This is the one. You'll love it." Poppy spoke mostly with her hands. All fell under her spell.

Afterwards, Jen stayed behind to help David clean up. She savoured the quietness of the now empty room. Wine glasses clinked together as she carried them out into his kitchen. Even though she washed and dried them, he was still annoyed. Poppy lingered too, watching Jen move the furniture to its original setting.

"Are you coming next week? It will be at my house," Poppy teased.

"Yes, along as it's ok with Rob," Jen promised.

"Great, I look forward to it." Poppy smiled, letting her gaze linger and reached inside her bag for her copy, creased and yellowed with age. "You can borrow mine."

Poppy had left behind her scarf of beautiful silk. Jen picked it up, brought it to her face, and took in a deep breath. It felt like she was holding Poppy close to her, never wanting to let go.

***

At the following week's book club, Jen knew she had been talking for too long, but she couldn't stop. This time they held their meet in Poppy's home, Jen felt all warm and cosy. She never wanted this evening to end.

David and the others were growing impatient to air their thoughts, but it was clear Poppy only cared about her point of view.

"It just really spoke to me. It was like this book had been written just for me. I am Jane Eyre. And at the end, he didn't marry her, she married him. Women can be strong, even when they have nothing." Was this why Poppy has chosen it?

David huffed and offered some small comment only audible to him.

"This book saved me when I was lonely, going through my divorce." Poppy placed her hand on Jen's knee.

"I think it's time for another coffee." David announced, breaking their moment apart.

Jen waited behind on the sofa when the others left to gather their things. She held out Poppy's scarf, not wanting to give it back. "You left this at David's last week."

Poppy took it. "Oh yes, so I did." She reached for it and left it on the sofa, already forgotten.

"May I use your bathroom?" Jen couldn't think of anything else to say to stay a little longer before she had to return home.

"Upstairs, second on the left."

No one else had been allowed to go upstairs. Poppy had made them make do with the small toilet under the stairs. She held her breath up the stairs, feeling naughty, like a child eavesdropping on the adult world. When Jen passed Poppy's bedroom, she couldn't resist having a quick look.

The walls were lilac, the curtains draped. The carpet soft like grass under her feet. Everything pristine. Her vision fluttered; the air was heavy with the scent of deep red roses. She breathed in as much as she could until she felt caught in an embrace.

Jen wanted to stay here forever. It was a room you'd find in a witch's cottage, deep in the wilds, standing outside of time. She felt protected here. If only she could escape the world of man. She walked over to the dressing table, wanting to see what perfume Poppy wore on her skin dotted with freckles the colour of honeycomb.

Lodged in the seam between the mirror and frame was an old calling card.

Do you feel all alone with your troubles and no one to talk to? Then ring this number. I'll eat your pain away.

It was very old, the number listed an out of date calling code for London. Thirty years at least. Jen rang the number and got through straight away.

***

A few hours later. Jen came downstairs, her limbs unsteady as a newborn lamb as she leaned against the wall to keep her upright. She hadn't remembered drinking any wine. "Poppy, I'm so sorry. I must have fallen asleep?"

"You must be so awfully tired from it all," Poppy observed, she was in the living room reading by her art deco Tiffany lamp.

Outside it was dark, the stars were out but had been pulled down until they were uncharacteristically bright and large.

Poppy put her book down. "Are you free tomorrow, during the day? I thought we could do yoga or go for a walk somewhere nice. Let's watch the leaves fall."

Jen smiled, her headache forgotten. "I'd love that."

***

They opted for a walk in their local park. Hazy golden sunlight drifted down to the forest floor. Birds sung up high, squirrels leapt from branch to branch. The white noise of the city around them gone. Poppy got to meet Beatrix and marveled at how lovely she was. At least Jen was doing something right. Rob couldn't say no as he was at work. It didn't take long for Poppy to prize Jen open. She was a voracious reader and now she set her eyes on Jen.

"I gave it all up when I had baby Bea. I thought it sounded nice, being a lady of leisure. I never enjoyed working. Never got paid much and I was always the one who got picked on. I've never been good at anything and now I have no money. I'm completely reliant on him."

"Can't you find something part-time? I don't mind baby-sitting." Already Poppy was such a good friend. It had been years since she'd had one.

"Well, I asked if I could get some shifts down at the local supermarket, all the other mums from my baby group work there.

But Rob said no. He says I'm being greedy. Someone else worse off than me would be denied a job all because I wanted a little pocket money."

Poppy stopped walking and stood still. "How do you get by with no money and no freedom?"

Jen came under the shadow of an oak tree. Her eyes began to sting. She hadn't wanted to end up like this. Jen used to be proud of herself, but Rob had pushed her down this path and she saw no way off it. "I'm not."

Poppy held out her arms. Jen didn't hesitate; she fell straight into them, resting her head on Poppy's shoulder. The sudden surge of intimacy made her afraid. She didn't deserve kindness. She had always been led to believe she was a terrible person, a waste of space.

It unleashed everything she had been holding onto. "He was lovely at the beginning, but I must have changed. He's always stood by me though. Even when, last year when I bought a lipstick for our anniversary, he went berserk. He found the purchase on the receipts. I have to give him all the receipts. I thought it was an OCD thing, but I think he just wants complete control."

"How long have you been married?"

"Well, that's the thing. He won't marry me. He says he might as well sign his life away. *If you leave me, you'll get the lot, everything I've worked so hard for.*" She stood up straight and looked Poppy in the eye. "The house is in his name, even the savings."

"Jen, you can't live like this, look at what it's doing to you."

"He only lets me go to book club because David is his friend." In a very quiet voice, she didn't realise she possessed. "I can't leave him."

"No, you can't." Poppy never failed to shock Jen. Usually at this point she would have been told how she was a strong confident woman who could do anything she put her mind to. "If you leave, you'll have nothing, and you know he'll find you. He'll find a way to take Bea from you."

"I know."

***

Rob had said Jen could host Book Club when it came to her turn. He bid a retreat upstairs with a four pack of Stella when the doorbell began to chime. Though he briefly came down to shake David's hand, he purposely ignored everyone else.

Jen thought she saw Poppy baring her teeth at Rob when they passed one another in the hallway. Fortunately, Rob hadn't noticed. In an unguarded moment, it looked as if Poppy possessed preternaturally sharp teeth, but Jen concluded the shadows she stood in must have been playing tricks.

Poppy and Jen occupied the small sofa and together they led the book group. Everyone had fun. It was Poppy who brought round the wine which she served straightaway. Glasses were constantly topped throughout the evening. Jen felt a thrill to be getting intoxicated behind Rob's back.

It had been years since she'd felt this giddy. Never again would anyone see the wild woman she had once been. The thought was sobering. She had been to university and built up a reputation for being reckless, but her clothes she now wore, bought by Rob, squashed all that. Her and Alison had been formidable together. She missed her each day.

In her relationships there was always a bargain to be wrestled over, give and take, compromise and defeat. Holding her voice whilst the other spoke. Delicately negotiating little matters, trying to stay sane and remember who she was before. But with a true friend, there was just support, ears that listened, a voice that spoke the truth, and wine, there was always wine and perfect trust. Someone who would notice when her hair looked great, or that something was not quite right underneath. They would notice her absence like a missing tooth. They'd ring in the middle of the night. They would know all her secrets just as she knew theirs, yet they both would still hold mysteries to one another. She could laugh with them until her belly became tight, and cry until her sorrow had bled out. Friends ate each other's pain in a way no lover ever could.

Why did she stop having fun? Because she thought she ought

to settle down and that was what women did when they got older. They sacrificed themselves for the good of their family. She settled down from fear of being left alone once people retreated from the party of youth.

But now she saw there was something worse than being alone, being kept a prisoner. She was not allowed to be herself, not allowed to evolve with the years. She must always be the same woman Rob found all those years ago. Keep the same interests even though she had outgrown them. She wanted to walk around the city, peruse secondhand book shops, go see a play or two, meet friends for coffee. Have good sex.

"Hang in there," Poppy whispered in her ear. The room spun around her, and she didn't mind one bit.

***

When she awoke, the others had gone. The room was cold against her. If Poppy had gone, she might have to go for a whole week without seeing her. But some sense told her to go upstairs.

A soft, contented sigh cradled her ears as Jen passed her baby girl's room. Upstairs, the hallway was dark except for the pale light coming from their bedroom. Her stomach heaved, he always wanted sex when drunk and not the kind a woman liked. She prayed he would sleep until morning. Hopefully his hangover would keep him subdued so she could have a day off, unless his temper rose.

Jen slowly nudged open their door. The TV was on low, casting out a blue glow rising and falling as it glared against their walls. Rob, in a drunken stupor, lay on the bed, limbs outstretched like the Vitruvian Man.

Poppy hadn't gone home with the others; she sat astride Rob, looking down with intent. When Jen came closer, Poppy smiled and crouched down until her face was so close to Rob's, she could pull him into a kiss.

Rob was her man, but Jen felt nothing. Their relationship died long ago. *Take him*, she thinks, *you'll be doing me a favor.* Poppy looked behind her to Jen, her eyes shifting, turning dark and feral.

"Is this what you want?" Poppy asked, her throat raspy.

Jen nodded.

Poppy's mouth opened wide, and from inside her gullet came the screams of the previous sources of pain. Jen edged closer to the bed. She wasn't afraid. Rob opened his eyes, becoming unusually alert for someone so drunk. Something inside him had told him what was about to happen.

But he had already been pinned down.

His head was the first bite. Poppy clamped down. Her jaws bellowing open until they matched those of a great white. She suckled the head, absorbed the flesh, as bones both small and large crunched. The white, ungiving cartilage and springy tendons chewed apart. Like a string of spaghetti, she sucked the rest of him down.

Nothing remained. Jen relaxed her shoulders and cried, but this time they were of joy. She didn't have to be that downtrodden woman anymore, now she was free.

Poppy leaned back, sounding like a mother bird regurgitating her haul, yet this time she was taking it all down into herself. The pain of the world, bite by bite. Her body expanding like a python as it digested. Her form silhouetted against the darkness. Her eyes watered with the strain. Jen held out her hand and placed it on Poppy's shoulder. True friends were so hard to find.

When Poppy turned to her, her eyes were bloodshot, tears of red running down, but it wasn't her blood. She smiled and grinned like the satiated wolf alone in the deep dark woods. Her teeth were unnaturally sharp. From inside, Jen heard Rob's ignored screams as he battled to get out. His fear becoming her strength.

Poppy let out a long sigh, the smell of Rob's aftershave that made Jen feel sick, the tang of sour beer breath.

It was done.

Poppy was exhausted but happy, and she nestled down on the bed where Rob used to sleep, now the space was hers. She stretched out and then curled up under the duvet. Jen beside her stroked her hair as she fell asleep. They would be friends forever.

Amazing Offer!

THE KING OF THE BEACH

by Patrick Barb

Tide came in, saltwater stretching to the dunes and washing away the sandcastles, but nobody found any trace of the Pencil-Neck Geek. "See?" Hudson said, trying to get Sheriff Jenny's attention. "Doesn't this prove I didn't have nothing to do with the Penc…his disappearance?"

The crescent moon hid behind the clouds. Every flashlight's beam was trained on waterlogged sand and shells. As a result, Hudson couldn't properly gauge the sheriff's reaction. Bad enough she hadn't stopped and listened to him when he talked. Or even when the whole disappearing nerd show kicked off. If she had, things probably wouldn't have escalated the way they did.

Lacking a time machine to right those wrongs, Hudson moved closer, ready to repeat himself and make sure his words were acknowledged. The sheriff must've been damn fast, with her boots' thick soles resisting the wet sand slurry sucking on her heels, because her light shone in the teenager's eyes and put him on the back foot quickly. "Hey! You…" Hudson started.

But he bit his tongue and didn't tell her what he really thought about her. He could've done it. *And I wouldn've blamed myself for it either. But who knows? Maybe I'm a better man than most.*

Sheriff Jenny didn't share the same opinion. "Be grateful I haven't had one of my deputies put you in a holding cell down at the station while we sort this mess out, son. Now, get outta my face."

She stomped off, calling out commands to the search party. Hudson was left blinking, trying to get rid of the little black dots in his peripheral vision.

Black dots like grains of sand.

Hudson Parrish believed the old sheriff, Sheriff A.T. Charles, was a good lawman. There was a fellow who understood who was worth listening to and who was worth believing. Hudson's daddy said Sheriff Jenny, Deputy Jenny back then, got inside everybody's head about Sheriff Charles. She had everyone convinced it was a bad thing if he borrowed a little money seized from the stoners, wasteoids, and dropouts he busted buying, selling, and using drugs under the boardwalk, then spent the same dirty money on himself and his family.

What, like they'd spend the money any better?

No drugs for Hudson. No, sir. No dope, no smoke, no poke. Matter-of-fact, Hudson called himself "Mr. No Supplements". He got his Greek demi-god body—with zero-percent body fat, and muscles stacked on top of muscles—the old-fashioned way: through hard work. Without the hard work of eating from his daddy's dietician-approved meal-plan and following the exercise program crafted by the family's trainer, Tino, Hudson knew he couldn't have achieved the level of perfection he'd reached. Hudson was a self-made man, a King of the Beach.

Without self-dedication (and the blessings of the good Lord above), Hudson might've ended up like the Pencil-Neck Geek and been the one *getting* the sand kicked in his face. Instead of the one kicking…

Of course, if it was me it happened to, I wouldn't get buried under some freak mountain of sand. I'd fight back.

Hudson considered following after the sheriff one last time, but the sound of sniffling behind him stopped the young man in his tracks. God only knew he'd gotten used to hearing this particular person's sobbing throughout the long day at the beach. So once he picked up on the sound, he stomped off across the gritty, pebbled segment of the sand, calling as he went, "Becca, is that you?"

She didn't answer, but her sniffling grew louder. "Bec—!"

Before Hudson finished, he found his quarry. Out in the dark, away from the search party spread across the beach, his knee struck the towel-covered back of the girl who'd pointed her finger at him. The way he figured it, Hudson believed she was as responsible for whatever happened to the Pencil-Neck Geek as everyone thought he was.

"Owww!" Becca's moan came like the slow release of air from a deflated balloon.

Hudson fought back the urge to put his hand over her mouth. He did need her to keep quiet after all. He took a deep breath and knelt in the sand. His breath came out and ruffled the soft charcoal-black hair on the girl's head.

"Hi," he said, fixing a smile on his face. "I hoped we could talk about what happened."

With mascara running down her cheeks and a quivering frown forming on her lips, Becca Gray wasn't anyone's idea of beautiful, at least as far as Hudson was concerned. And her words were worse. "Get away from me. You killed him. You killed Mackenzie."

"Whoa, whoa, whoa!" Hudson held his hands up, palms out. "I didn't kill that Pencil-Ne…Mackenzie…Mac, whatever his name was."

Becca shook her head, wet strands of hair slapping against her forehead.

"He never did anything to you."

***

Except it wasn't true. Not the way Hudson remembered it. After all, it was hard to forget when some ninety-pound weakling managed to ruin a perfectly awesome day at the beach.

It started so normally too. Hudson and the boys—Jaxon, Jordan, Jamal, and Javier—were throwing the pigskin around. Everybody kept trying to one-up each other, putting more and more distance between them with each pass. And Hudson wouldn't let any of the four Jays get the better of him. So he became the one running faster, reaching farther, making sure everyone around knew he was the best. *The King.*

Javier, the second-string QB, cocked back his throwing arm and launched a Hail Mary bomb arcing below the sun. Hudson waited, counting one, two, three, before he took off across the sand. It was perfect. Sprinting backward at top speed, Hudson felt everyone's eyes on his progress. The kids building castles, the moms pretending to watch the kids building castles but really watching him. They all stopped to take in the majesty of the King of the Beach.

As Javier's near-perfect spiral began its descent and Hudson stretched out his arms, he was certain his adoring admirers were set to witness another picture-perfect catch. *I can do it all*, Hudson thought.

Of course, he'd missed out on the duo sitting under their massive umbrella, hiding from the sun like a pair of vampiric ghouls. He'd missed the boy—a scrawny thing with ribs showing through his skin so pale it was like a corpse's—stretching out across the sand, his straw-thin hair in his eyes.

What was he even reaching for in the sand anyway?

Whatever Mackenzie *had* stretched across the ratty beach blanket for, he never had a chance to grab it. And Hudson never had a chance to grab Javier's imperfect pass, never got to pull it down from the sky and hold it against his pecs.

The back of his leg struck the side of Mackenzie's neck. For a split second, Hudson's gaze dropped. Met with the Pencil-Neck Geek's face twisted in agony, the King of the Beach recoiled.

And dropped the ball.

The sand splashed up, hitting Mackenzie in the face and splattering Hudson's calf. Nothing more than a few grains of sand catapulted from a beach made of thousands, millions of grains of sand.

Once everything settled, silence followed. For Hudson, the silence lasted a lifetime. The winds picked up, pushing the heady aroma of dead fish, saltwater, and seagull droppings up his nose. And with the whistling breezes, he was certain he picked up the "oohs" of his teammates.

But not the good "oohs," not the admiring, fawning "oohs."

Hudson couldn't stare across the beach for his friends' reactions. He didn't want to face whatever waited for him. If failure was a disease, he'd rather quarantine himself and avoid spreading further contamination. Instead of picking up the ball from its spot on the ground, where the oval-shaped brown mass rocked back and forth, burning off the momentum of Javier's throw, Hudson trained his eyes on the one who'd made him miss the catch. The catch he should've made. The catch he would've made. If it hadn't been for…

"You!" Hudson's cry was both reproach and the best he could manage when it came to remembering the name of the weirdo kid he'd tripped over.

For his part, the weirdo kid was rubbing the side of his face. Spreading the white, brown, black, and red tiny rocks making up the beach sand against his cheek. Like it was a salve. Looking back, Hudson considered it the moment he should've backed off. Should've jogged down the beach, laughing off the catch he definitely would've made otherwise. *Can you believe that Pencil-Neck Geek made me miss?"*

But that wasn't what happened.

"You made me miss," he repeated to the sniveling skeletal specimen kneeling before him in the sand.

"It was an accident, Hudson." His eyes flicked across to the pale nothing of a girl on the beach blanket.

She'd look a whole lot better if she smiled, he thought, before returning his attention to more pressing matters.

"I'm sorry…I'm…" The Pencil-Neck Geek's rubbing turned into full-on scratching. His untrimmed fingernails dug into the sallow flesh on his cheeks. Hudson's eyes widened as the grains of sand fell between the bloody openings.

He took a step back, a tingling sensation racing through his body. His heart pounded a millisecond faster than normal.

Hudson Parrish never worried about his well-being, never fretted about what any given day held for him. The answers were always the same after all. So the new sensation stopped Hudson in his tracks. It disrupted his train of thought, like a squirrel running across the rail lines into an oncoming locomotive. He bit his lip, swallowing back a stuttered protest.

The Jays appeared, moving closer, their silhouettes glimmering like mirages under the noon-time beach sun. They moved as this perfect, chiseled, oiled unit. One entity ready to stand in judgment of its King.

Fear? Was that it?

Hudson didn't have time for introspective, touchy-feely questions. He was a young man of action and, by definition, he needed to act.

"You, Pencil-Neck Geek! Watch where you're going on *my* beach!" As though to punctuate his declaration, Hudson drew back his foot—ignoring the low-level throbbing from where he'd made contact with the side of the so-called Pencil-Neck Geek's sand-deckled head—then shot it forward. Spreading his toes on impact, increasing the surface area covered by his kick.

He'd expected a slight spray of fine-grained beach sand. Something to get caught in the other boy's eyelashes, nostrils, and the moist quivering "O" of his fishy lips. It would be another picture-perfect moment, a showcase for Hudson's obvious superiority and dominance. The Jays would bear witness to his triumph, and all would be well in the world once more.

The shrill cry of the goth girl, with her black swimsuit covering her skin like an oil spill, making it impossible to evaluate her figure, broke apart Hudson's triumphant vision of his near future before he had a chance to live in it.

At his feet, Mackenzie the Pencil-Neck Geek, the interloper on Hudson's beach, the interrupter of Hudson's moment of triumph, threw up his hands. He screamed, though to Hudson's ear it sounded more like a squeal, the frightened whine of a pig taken to slaughter.

The wave of sand crested above the mewling boy's head. Stretching out a few feet lengthwise, the sand rose to Hudson's chest. The tanned and fit perfect specimen of young American masculinity gritted his teeth against the blowback of sand particles against his body. Later, he'd steal a towel from some shocked onlooker and wipe away sand and thin rivulets of blood from around his nipples.

But it came after the sand fell. Like the rolling waves down by the shoreline, battering the wet sand squished between the toes of those preparing to frolic in the saltwater, the sand kicked up by Hudson had to crash eventually.

It fell onto the Pencil-Neck Geek. Not breaking apart on impact, grains spread wide across the boy's nearly prone form. The sand-maintained cohesion moved as a unit, so it was more like Hudson had kicked some gritty blanket or funeral shroud over the kid. The King of the Beach lost his balance, falling backward.

His rear-end hit the ground and the sand wave enveloped the Pencil-Neck Geek in its gritty embrace.

And then, he was gone.

The girl launched herself out from under their umbrella as though someone had struck a match by her face. At least it explained the redness flushing her cheeks like some high-temperature fever and the wide-eyed panic filling her eyes.

Hudson sat in the sand, watching as the girl tore through the gritty remnants of the wave he'd kicked up and that'd buried her companion. She dug her fingers into the sand, sifting it through her black marker-painted nails. The grains fell as though passing through an hourglass. A steady drizzle ticking away seconds, minutes.

I don't understand. Where'd he go?

The girl stood, letting more sand fall from between her fingers. She shuffled to the spot where Hudson had kicked the sand. She rubbed the ground flat, smooth. Then her heels dug deeper furrows. But there was nothing left of the Pencil-Neck Geek.

Hudson picked out the Jays, closer than they'd been before he kicked the sand. He swore he saw their eyes narrow, saw them whispering between each other. Telling secrets, embracing dissension. Then, they faded into the background. Slinking away from the stink of danger, of failure, Hudson felt something throbbing inside.

Go on then, he thought. *Leave me, you cowards!*

He'd never admit how much it hurt to watch them leave.

The girl crawled across the flattened sand, no trace of the boy buried under it. As though he'd never been there in the first place. As though Hudson had done nothing more than kick sand on top of more sand. Her hands, gripping Hudson's shoulders, were cold and clammy like she'd washed them in ice water.

"What did you do?" she asked.

"What did I…what did I…"

*****

After the onlookers rose from their beach towels, the lifeguards descended from their white-painted perches, the sheriff and her deputies drove their All-Wheel Drive vehicles across the sand, and the beach was cleared (except for those involved in the "incident"), Hudson still found himself lost for answers to a question he couldn't even articulate.

What did I do?

As Becca scooted across the sand, dragging the edge of the towel through the grains, Hudson found what he believed to be his source of truth slithering away from him. Like a snake. And yet, he couldn't reach out and grab her. These days there was always the chance someone would take things the wrong way, get the wrong impression. If the Jays had stuck around, they could've helped him. They worked well together. Like a team, on the field, at the beach, in the hallways of their high school fiefdom.

But they'd gone. Abandoned him. Hudson only had himself to rely on. *Maybe it's dark enough. Maybe no one will notice me. And even if they do, what will they say? Who will they believe?*

He stretched out, hands prepared to wrap around her limbs and pull her up from the dunes. "Come here…"

But she didn't.

Twin plumes of sand shot up into the night sky, appearing on either side of the girl's prone form. Gravity appeared out of commission at the moment, the erupting sand swirled instead of falling pitter-patter against the ground. Becca's face showed shock and fear under the thin glow of moonlight glinting off twinkling sand grains.

Her fingers pressed against the sand beneath her. But they slipped under, as though turned to a swirling slurry of mud. And then the pale arms of her old friend wrapped around her black swimsuit. Her eyes widened. Nostrils flared. Finally, she looked to Hudson.

About time, he thought.

But there wasn't time for the self-satisfied gloating he'd otherwise embrace. Her whispered request sounded like a scream. "Help me."

Hudson stood and watched. His hands hung as leaden weights by his sides.

The emerging arms belonged to Pencil-Neck Geek. Still rail thin, his blue veins traced pathways up and down the limbs. They squeezed around the girl and the sand gave way below. She folded in on herself, legs pulled up to her shoulders until her body disappeared beneath the sand, up to her neck. Below the sand, something cracked. Like the report of a pistol.

Hudson looked away. *Looking for help*, he told himself. *Someone had to hear. Sheriff Jenny and her deputies will come and help.*

It wasn't that he was too scared to watch the blood trickle from the broken girl's nose and mouth. Nothing like that.

When he did look back, she was gone. Under the sand, the black marker nail polish on one finger was all he glimpsed. Then, nothing.

Ripples in the sand, as though someone shook a bedsheet, made shifting hills and valleys under Hudson's feet. *What's Daddy gonna say?* he wondered.

He'd called his old man when the Pencil-Neck Geek first went under the sand. But dear old Dad was like all the rest. He wouldn't listen. He didn't say it outright, but Hudson could reach between his father's words and find the unasked questions. "Are you on drugs? Another pathetic druggie hanging under the boardwalk, chasing dragons and hiding from pink elephants? Have you poisoned your perfect body?"

That's not it though, Daddy. That's not it at all. I didn't do anything to him. It was the sand. It was the beach.

The Pencil-Neck Geek pulled himself out of the sand, arms twisting back behind his head like some marionette contortionist, his inhumanly limber body under control by forces far beyond. A mini tornado of sand sprayed up into Hudson's face. He swatted the grains of sand as they hit him at full force. The cumulative effect of the high-speed impact carved a path of destruction across his face.

Blood fell like spilled oil, black and thick in the sand.

The Pencil-Neck Geek's fingers strummed against the ground. The sand hardened to a thick cement, so the boy's ra-tum, ra-tum became like the ticking beat of a metronome.

Hudson smeared blood and sand from his eyes. Tears made up the last ingredient in the medley. They stuck to his chin like his daddy's five o'clock shadow. Like he was a little kid playing dress-up, smearing Mommy's make-up on and calling himself a "handsome young man."

The face staring at him was a familiar one. But it was wrong.

The Pencil-Neck Geek stood before Hudson, and he was all wrong. The pale, blue-tinted skin was gone, replaced with gray sand the color of the static test pattern on an old TV set. The eyebrows were the bones of fish, picked nearly bare by the scavenger seabirds. The eyes staring right into Hudson's soul were shattered seashell remnants. Ancient fossils ground to nothing. The leering grin was sodden algae, washed up to the dunes. This sandman facsimile of humanity stared at Hudson. It watched him. It judged him.

The tiny trinkets used for facial features fell off one by one. Until nothing remained but the sand. Hudson opened his mouth to speak, to scream, to do something.

But the boy made of sand collapsed. His sand returned to the beach. When Hudson looked down, he found the same awful smirk magnified one hundred-fold. The dunes themselves formed cheeks, a nose, and a mouth. Like some mosaic in the sand, the Pencil-Neck

Geek was beautiful when blown up that way.

Like a door slammed closed in his mind, a loud clap and the sudden absence of light took over Hudson's senses. When he came to, the Pencil-Neck Geek waited for him. One more kid he never noticed. Another shrimpy weakling. The sun rose behind them, the morning star's rays like a crown over the pathetic boy's head.

"Look at me," he said. "Look at me," the Pencil-Neck Geek named Mackenzie repeated.

"Listen, Mac…" but Hudson never finished. He looked and he saw.

Pale blue eyes melting to sand. Pouring out of Mackenzie's sockets. Out of his mouth. Sand falling, falling.

Hudson dropped to the ground as well, averting his eyes but opening his mouth. The grit of sand moved past his perfect lips, through his perfect teeth, down his perfect esophagus, all to fill his perfect stomach. He moaned in ecstatic reverence. He dug his fingers under the sand and shells and seaweed. He let baby hermit crabs burrow into the sand beneath his nails, pressing them up off the nailbeds on his fingers.

He bled into the sand and paid his homage. There was a new King of the Beach and Hudson would do whatever it took to find favor in the new kingdom to come.

MISS RHEINGOLD 1956

by Nicholas Alexander Hayes

Will the real Miss Rheingold please stand out –
cheeks of apples and marshmallow fluff –
blonde and rather puffy, with the quality
of a prettiness that could not provoke
distinction?

Mayfly maiden, barfly elect –
clone of temperate desire,
domestic mimicry, and civic simulation.

Sexless in a heavy dress.
Bare neck and face
emerging from fur collar.

Joyless smile
holding a pachyderm
and jackass.

Never bitter, never sweet –
always clean and crisp.

No Fixed Abode

by Ben Walker

Jonno scraped at the change in his hand, sliding the coins around his palm with one finger, as if rubbing the dull metal discs together would somehow cause them to multiply, like a sleight-of-hand trick. The cashier watched him, no trace of patience on their otherwise expressionless face. After a few painful moments of store muzak and the grating of metal on metal, the cashier cleared their throat.

"One second," Jonno said.

"If you haven't got the money—"

"One. Second," Jonno repeated. "*Please.*" He hoped desperation hadn't cracked his voice, but from the look on the cashier's face, it had. Small wonder. This was the lowest point of his life thus far. Addiction had rooted itself in his system like a weed these past few years, cutting off his common sense, starving him of rational thought. His only desire was to get as fucked up as possible, and the bottle currently tipped over on the store's conveyor belt was his last chance for that until payday. That was in two days. The hand sanitizer cost $2. He had $1.50.

"There are other people in line, sir."

With a frustrated snarl, Jonno slammed his money down onto the belt. "This is all I have."

The clerk looked down at the change. Back up at Jonno. Sympathy softened their gaze. They scooped up the money and dumped it into the register.

"Do you need a bag?"

***

All Jonno needed was a moment alone with the tiny container. The alcohol percentage was far higher than most of the actual drinks he could find, let alone afford. One extra benefit was the acrid *lasting citrus freshness* the packaging promised, an easy way to deflect attention and suspicion. Not that he aroused either of them most days; just another face in a crowd of people too busy to notice one another's problems, much less care about how wasted someone was at three PM on a Saturday. Making his way across the parking lot to the street beyond, Jonno fumbled with his purchase as he fished his keys out from his pocket.

Home sweet home, he thought, sliding the key into the rust-specked door of his '83 Miser. The lock never opened right the first time, but it wasn't like he had any pressing engagements, any reason to worry about the speed of his entry. After a few jiggles he was in, shaded by the trees above, ready to slip into sweet oblivion for as long as his body would allow.

Idle notions of home drifted through his mind as he wrestled with the tamper seal on the lurid yellow bottle. Nervous excitement bubbled in his belly as he brought the bottle to his mouth. The first sting of lemon-infused chemicals seeped into his blistered lower lip, then—

Tap. Tap.

Jonno's nerves caused him to smack the hard plastic against his gums, a dull wave of pain shooting through his mouth. A spitty dribble of gel escaped down his salmon-coloured shirt, leaving a snail trail behind which he didn't bother to wipe.

The knocks came again, more insistent. Keeping as steady a grip on the bottle as he could, Jonno flipped the cap shut and turned to face the window.

There stood an ashen person, their features mostly obscured by a jaunty blue hat, peaked with a shiny leather brim. In the shade, Jonno could just about see their pockmarked chin. The rest of their getup was more easily identifiable than their features. Blue suit. Satchel over one shoulder. A postal worker.

The person gave a wan smile, as slight as the store clerk's, then raised a clammy-looking fist, the knuckles bone-white, and rapped on the window one more time. When Jonno didn't react, they circled one finger around in the air: *wind the window down.*

Jonno shook his head, the jittery motion spreading to every part of his body. "You've made a mistake," he said, no authority in his tone. His unwanted visitor was a long way from any kind of residential area. Nowhere close to a post office. Come to think of it, the ashen figure's clothing didn't seem to gel with the modern era either, all pressed neat lines and shiny buttons instead of the comfy shorts and sweat-stained armpits he was used to seeing on the local post-people.

The ashen postal worker moved close enough to fog the window with its breath as it spoke. "Jonathan Connolly." Statement, not question. There had been no mistake. They knew damn well who he was.

Still, Jonno shook his head.

"I need you to sign for this, young Master Connolly. Formerly of one-zero-seven, West Juniper Lane." They spoke like a game show host; congenial out of obligation.

Jonno shook his head again, softer. Forty years. Forty goddamn years since his parents had taken in that package. No amount of gut-rot had ever washed away that scrap of memory, to kill that piece of his brain. Tears formed in Jonno's eyes as he stared blankly ahead, refusing to acknowledge the ashen one, nor the memories threatening to sprout as a result of their words.

"So many forwarding addresses since then. Shall I go on, young Master Connolly? Thricewood Young Boy's Home. Not too keen on visitors there, but the post must prevail. Then once we're of age, we become Master Connolly, don't we, resident at number seven Shepshed Gardens. That apartment was a fine set-up. Glendale, wasn't it? Not exactly a gated community, your landlord was a bit too obliging when it came to deliveries, hmm? Then things get messy for a while, young offender's institutions, the halfway house. Locked down tight. Assumed identities, not to mention protection from what was assumed to be wrong with your young mind. So fortunate to have stayed out of the wards, really. And speaking of fortune, we come to our last known address. Eighty-five Keystone Avenue. Such kindness there from – what was his name?"

Jonno sobbed. That was Michael's house. Jonno's first home with anyone he'd truly loved since that first delivery. Michael had been so generous with his love, his sympathy. And yet for all the wounds Jonno had opened up, had allowed him to see, it wasn't enough. Michael hadn't listened. Not really. Nobody ever did.

"Yes," the ashen figure said, hissing out the *s*. "Trust is so hard to find, so much harder to lose. And so we come to your little road trip. No fixed abode. Close to a decade of frustration on our end. But you see, 'not at this address' is less of a statement to us, and more of a challenge."

With that. the ashen one dipped its hand into the satchel at its side and brought out a small parcel. As lovingly as a mother might stroke a child's hair, it placed the six-inch square box on the bonnet of the Miser.

"No need to sign this time," they told Jonno. "We're past that now. Just...enjoy your delivery."

Jonno closed his eyes against the sting of his tears, hearing a rough scraping sound, like something unfurling, before a gust of wind blew a scattering of gravel up against the side of his car. Then, nothing. When he opened his eyes, he was staring right at the box. It was as if he'd purchased those stupid fake X-ray specs all those years back too. He could picture the shape of the item inside, right down to the last detail. More than that, he could see that reason had no place here, not now. There was only the box, and the promise it held.

He wept openly as he threw the hand sanitizer into the back seat, then nudged open the driver's side door with his knee. The words of the advert floated into his vision as if he were seeing them again for the first time some four decades prior.

***

Venus fly trap. As real as the real thing! Better even!

Jonno felt his gut twist with excitement at the black-and-white promise laid out at the back of his comic. Best of all, he'd receive

<u>*ten whole plants*</u> *guaranteed (while stocks last)*! Getting anything through the mail was a rare treat for a nine-year old. The problem was money, but his parents were far too doting to ever suspect him of dipping into his father's wallet *for the low, low price of just one dollar and fifty cents!*

He wrote so shakily on the form, printed and signed his name so illegibly he thought the parcel would never arrive. And despite the advertisement's promises that *satisfaction will be yours* and *delivery is guaranteed*, he forgot about his illicit purchase until it arrived. Months later, when the doorbell rang, he shouted for his mother to find out who, or what, was at the door.

***

Every day since had been a mission to forget. He'd prayed at first, and, when that didn't work, he'd clung hard to the notion that ignorance was bliss, trying anything he could to push his memories down into some forgotten corner of himself, to smother the flames of guilt. Every new package, each fresh tragedy had rekindled that fire. That burning was absent now, replaced with a hollowness accentuated by the steady throb of his pulse in his ear. He turned the box towards him, noticing that the address had been blacked out, the words *no fixed abode* scribbled on the cardboard beneath in cursive. Below that, a faded red stamp:
Cast iron satisfaction!

Whose satisfaction? Jonno wondered, idly thumbing at a loose piece of tape on the parcel's edge as he returned to the front seat of his car. There he sat, resting the package on his lap. It felt impossibly heavy against his thighs. His eyes went to the rear-view mirror where the reflection of the discarded sanitizer appeared. He could take a sip, forget all this for a while, but the box would always find him. He knew that now, just as he'd always known it.

Jonno dug his thumbnail into the tape at the box's neatly fastened top edge and slid it across, breaking the seal with ease. Reaching in, he pulled out the plant, still as vibrantly green as the day he'd found the first one on the doorstep, his mother's legs sticking out obscenely from its jaws. The rest of her had been contorted in impossible ways, her entire mass squeezed to fit down the plant's slender gullet. His father had tried, oh god had he tried to pull her away from the plant's hungry mouth, but once the old man's hand brushed against those trigger hairs, he was gone. Just as gone as all the others who'd ever accepted a delivery on his behalf; the curious and the ignorant, lovers and liars, all dead because of his weakness.

Jonno brushed the box aside and set the plant down on his lap, taking in its aroma. Fresh chlorophyll. Dew. Faint traces of copper.

He glanced at the sanitizer one more time, then stared back at the plant. Deep into its crimson-flecked mouth.

"As real as forgetting," he muttered. "Better, even."

He bent forwards in supplication, feeling the tender jaws stretch around his head, the digestive enzymes beginning to sting at his lips. With no trace of a smile, Jonno waited for the satisfaction he'd been promised.

THE SALTY MONKEY MYSTERY

by Ann Wuehler

Dahlia regarded the brown-paper wrapped package resting against her door frame. Ten hours cleaning at St. Mark's Hospital Center left a body past tired, left a mind numb and dull. She picked it up, the weight perhaps that of a handful of feathers. The return label said Harold Van Braunhunt, INC. A smiling half-monkey, half-fish creature regarded her, drawn by hand beneath the return label. Her address, machine-printed and stuck to the package. She turned the package over, mystified to her small, timid soul. What on earth was this?

Something splashed inside; the package had a squishy quality. Another prank? Life seemed full of those quite ready to prank Dahlia Marie Simpkins.

Inside her tiny studio apartment, the package rested on Dahlia's folding table where she ate her meals, worked on her quilting, and wrote her secret steamy stories she published under the name Stephanie Scandall. She had thirty-two followers on Storybook. One had even sent her a message that her tale of the centaur and the starfish girl had really rocked their world; 'funniest thing since death!' had been another actual comment. People could be awful and nice.

Perhaps this was a gift from an admirer?

But she had never written anything about monkeys or mermaids. How had Van Braunhunt gotten her home address? And how had a package been left at her apartment door? Packages were left with the manager, Mrs. Mabel Larsen, of the Oak Tree Apartment Complex. A mystery! A real one.

First thing, of course, was to open the package. What if it contained anthrax or some sort of weapon? The news daily reminded her that such things actually did happen. Dahlia's thoughts scattered and hid as something in the package rustled.

Something struck the paper and taped edges from the inside. The inside. She stepped back from her own table, reaching for her one good knife. Her mind settled, snapped, locked back into place.

How could it breathe?

Down went her knife, but she could reach it, just in case.

The paper tore with a true ease. A flat box had been used to house the contents. Her fingers hesitated about reaching into that package, about the size of a bag of frozen peas. She instead upended the package, letting the contents spill to the table's surface. Inside a sandwich bag with a zipped end floated a most strange and wondrous creature. About four to six inches in length, half of that length a violet and aquamarine fish tail, with alternating scales and long plumy ends like summer scarves. The other end seemed to be a monkey, with long monkey arms, a comical monkey face, giant bulging dark brown eyes that fixed on her with fear and pleading. Small curled brown feces bobbed in that filthy water. "What on earth?" Dahlia found her one good glass bowl, the one she used for Christmas when she bought clementines, placed them in the bowl, and tried to eat them all before they spoiled. It was her Christmas tradition, and a healthy one. But as it was past that holiday, the bowl had no other purpose at the moment.

First, she filled that clear glass bowl with tap water. The creature regarded her as she worked, before shaking its head. She noted a tiny sealed bag of what had to be table salt.

Indeed, it was. A baggie full of a monkey fish and a smaller baggie full of salt. A salt water gift from this Harold Van Braunhunt?

Oh.

Her fingers clutched the bowl's edges so hard she nearly broke it.

Had she not, when foolish, full of hope, young enough to have knees that yet worked, ordered sea monkeys from the back of a comic? A comic she'd tucked into her blouse at the Green Apple? Her one and only shoplifting adventure to please Abby Plowman, who had called her a chicken poop head. Not the exact words but cussing, really. When one had the entire English language at one's search engine? She had brought the comic to school the next day, but Abby pretended she had not dared Dahlia to steal it. You're a thief, and you're going to hell, Abby had said, the others laughing. Pointing, laughing, and Dahlia could only retreat, cry her cry in the bathroom stall. She had not told her dad or anyone.

Everyone always laughed.

Dahlia poured the little package of salt into the bowl of water. She stirred it with a spoon until it dissolved. "Are you a sea monkey?"

The big brown eyes regarded her, the wide mouth opened to reveal tiny sharp teeth, the webbed fingers pushed at the plastic baggie as it tried to avoid its own wastes.

"I ordered you years ago. And it's just brine shrimp. I looked that up. Sea monkeys are not actually monkeys," she said to her aquatic purchase from the way back time machine. Something mysterious and wonderful had happened here. Sometimes the universe cracked a bit, let weird things fall through. Yes. Of course.

She took up the baggie full of the lone sea monkey, who wiggled that gorgeous tail and swished about in the murky water, watching her rather anxiously. How strange to have a fish or whatever it was counting so on your kindness and ability to care for it at all. What did it eat? Did it sleep? Did it need some rocks, a bit of seaweed or a cattail? Plop into the bowl it went, and it fell straight to the bottom, gulping in that salted water with giant grateful gulps. She noted it had gills along each side, and fur. Very short fur, like a seal. Dark brown fur, with a splotch of gold here and there. No ears. A bald monkey-like pate. "Can you talk?"

It propelled itself upward, the head breaking the surface. A chitter that sounded like an alarm sent toward her. The creature sank back down, curling into a ball against the bottom. A webbed hand rubbed the belly. It glanced toward her, before closing those eyes, curling up even tighter, rather like a homeless man on a cold night. A starving homeless man.

"Do you eat meat? I have some baked chicken. I had it last

night."

Dahlia shook the package, and a small, folded note flew out. The monkey fish, or whatever it actually was, lifted its strangely primate head and blinked at her before it coiled up again, putting that spine to her, wrapping the tail about itself.

The note congratulated her on her purchase of a sea monkey. Unfortunately, she had only sent enough for one, and the company had graciously covered the postage due. Regular table salt, a teaspoon to a gallon of water, would do well enough to recreate the briny home the sea monkey needed to thrive. The sea monkey enjoys fish roe, but small amounts of raw or cooked meat would do in a pinch. She might also arrange some rocks for the sea monkey to use as a home and throw in some small pebbles for the sea monkey's amusement as they enjoyed arranging said pebbles in patterns when not napping or eating. Enjoy your new pet.

All of this hand-written, on letterhead with Harold Van Braunhunt at the top. No address or phone number or email.

A PS had been included.

Please forgive the unforgivable delay. Your order form slipped behind the cabinet. We did not find it until we did a deep clean. We aim to please, Dahlia Simpkins. Please accept further a second sea monkey, due in a week or so. We have paid to have it delivered to your current address. Your Uncle Barry assured us you lived there, as your Aunt Susan sent you a Christmas card this year.

Dahlia smoothed that astonishing note. The original order form. Her big sprawling handwriting, and yes, her dad's signature. Her dad had sent it off. Years ago.

Her eyes traveled to the garish red and lime green card her Aunt Susan had not even bothered to sign beyond her and Barry's names. Her one and only Christmas card this year.

The sea monkey accepted the bits of shredded, baked chicken. Dahlia also placed a chunk of obsidian in the bowl and the creature swam about it, before tugging it toward the left to hide behind it. She had almost fifty bucks saved up for emergencies. Her Dodge had broken down right before the holidays, emptying her small bank account with astonishing ease. Thrift stores might have an aquarium. If there was another one being sent, she'd need an aquarium. Maybe she could look up how to keep saltwater fish while researching pirates, her next steamy Stephanie Scandall project that she expected would take years to write. Her lips turned up in a happy smile at that prospect at being busy inventing tropical intrigues. Maybe she would do a small tropical quilt, blues and greens.

Purpose and projects.

Mrs. Larsen could not object to a fish tank. She might outlaw dogs and cats, but fish tanks had to be allowed. Dahlia geared herself up to ask if she could have a fish tank. Writing steamy heroines had given her a bit of courage. Having this small monkey fish thing had given her a bit of courage as well.

She had not sent in any money with that order.

Just the order, hastily filled out, stuffed into the past due envelope, with the address of the sea monkey place written above the see-through place where David Simpkin's name had gone. Her heart began to beat, her belly filled with sour tinglings. A twelve-year-old Dahlia had not had any money to send off for sea monkeys.

And yet, at nearly fifty, she had some sort of mashed together pet munching baked chicken while hiding behind the smooth obsidian fist-sized stone she had found while visiting her Aunt Susan for a summer in Drewsey, Oregon. Where her aunt had spoken to someone on a phone about not keeping Dahlia.

We just can't right now. We just can't.

A small webbed hand waved at her above the surface of the water.

Giant brown eyes stared at her in real worry. The plumy tail floated like streamers on a princess hat.

"Oh I'm fine, little friend," she said, not knowing what to call the fish. "Do you want some more chicken? I'll get an aquarium somehow. It will all work out, I promise."

The webbed hand waved at her and went below the water, the sea monkey now seated atop the obsidian, flipping those plumy fins up and down. She began to talk, as if it could understand her. A new chapter of her life had begun.

What a joy to hear the sea monkey splash about and gurgle and chitter at her once in a while as she worked on her new pirate project. When she went to bed that night, she set the bowl on the floor so the sea monkey would not have to be alone its first night.

ABOUT THE AUTHORS

Cindy O'Quinn is an Appalachian writer who grew up in the mountains of West Virginia. In 2016, Cindy and her family moved to the northern woods of Maine, where she continues to write horror stories and speculative poetry. Her work has been published or is forthcoming in *Shotgun Honey Presents Vol 4: RECOIL*, The Shirley Jackson Award Winning Anthology: *The Twisted Book of Shadows*, *Shelved: Appalachian Resilience During Covid 19* Anthology, *Attack From The '80s* Anthology, *The Bad Book* Anthology, *Chiral Mad 5*, *HWA Poetry Showcase Vol V*, *Space & Time Magazine*, *Weirdbook Magazine*, *Nothing's Sacred Vol 4 & 5*, *Sanitarium Magazine*, & others. Cindy is a two-time Bram Stoker Award Final Nominee. Her poetry has been nominated for both the Rhysling & Dwarf Star Awards. Member of HWA, NESW, NEHW, SFPA, Horror Writers of Maine, and Weird Poets Society. You can follow Cindy for updates on:

Facebook: @CindyOQuinnWriter, Instagram: cindy.oquinn, and Twitter @COQuinnWrites.

Catherine McCarthy is a spinner of stories with macabre melodies. She is the author of the collections *Door and other twisted tales* and *Mists and Megaliths*, and the novella *Immortelle* (Off Limits Press). Her Gothic novel, *A Moonlit Path of Madness*, will be published by Nosetouch Press in 2023. Her short fiction has been published by Brigids Gate Press, *Dark Matter Magazine*, Dark Recesses Press and Black Spot Books. When she is not writing she may be found hiking the Welsh coast path or huddled among ancient gravestones reading Machen or Poe. Discover more at:

https://www.catherine-mccarthy-author.com/ or at
https://twitter.com/serialsemantic

Sarah Jane Huntington is a hospice nurse who loves horror and science fiction. She spends her time reading, writing, watching movies and walking her dog. She is the author of four short story collections, one novel and one novella, and her work has appeared in several anthologies.

Simon Clarke lives and writes in Norfolk, United Kingdom. He enjoys writing fiction and poetry and has been published by Hedgehog Press, Black Hare Press, Breaking Rules Publishing, Fifty Word Stories, Breaking Rules Publishing Europe, Nothing Ever Happens In Fox Hollow and Prolific Press. He regularly submits to UK and international and is currently working on his first novel. He loves Gothic literature and all things mystical and mysterious.

https://linktr.ee/sclarkenp

A.E. Fiori lives in sunny Southern California, where she has been writing stories since she could put pen to paper. An author of sci-fi and fantasy, she loves using her anthropology degree for inspiration. It's those little details - most recently they can be seen in her work for Wyngraf. You can usually find her at home with her family and her dog, Watson. Visit her online at aefiori.com or follow her on Twitter at @aefiori.

Patricia Miller is a US Navy veteran born and raised in Cincinnati, Ohio, USA, a mostly retired IT Type with a BS from Miami University, Oxford, Ohio and an MS in Library and Information Science from the University of Tennessee. She started reading at 3 1/2 after becoming obsessed with Batman. She is hooked on QI, British murder villages and professional cycling.

Allen Ashley is a British Fantasy Award winner. He works as a developmental editor and creative writing tutor and is the founder of the advanced science fiction and fantasy group Clockhouse London Writers. He writes regularly for *Focus* of the British Science Fiction Association journal, and the *BFS Journal* from the British Fantasy Society. His most recent book is the poetry collection *Echoes from an Expired Earth* (Demain Publishing, UK, paperback 2021 – also available on Amazon). Further details at: www.allenashley.com.

Edward Barnfield is a writer and researcher living in the Middle East. His stories have appeared in *Ellipsis Zine, Lunate, Strands, Janus Literary, Leicester Writes, Cranked Anvil,* and *Reflex Press,* among others. In 2021, he won the Exeter Literary Festival and Bay Tales short story prizes. He's on Twitter at @edbarnfield.

N S Ford is a book fanatic, blogger and cat lover who lives in the UK with her family. She is the author of *We Watch You,* a dark psychological thriller with a speculative twist. When not reading or blogging, she juggles her writing time with parenting, working in heritage and playing the piano.

Website: https://nsfordwriter.com
Twitter: @nsfordwriter

Norbert Góra is a 32-year-old poet and writer from Poland. He is the author of more than 100 poems which have been published in poetry anthologies in USA, UK, India, Nigeria, Kenya and Australia.

Julie Sevens is a horror writer and an everything reader. The tentacular appendages of the universe have moved her from Ohio to Philadelphia, to Berlin. Now just beyond the interstellar blastzone of Chicago, Julie lives with her husband, two sons, a doorstep spider named Lentil, and a ghost in the closet who resists naming. Find more of her nightmares at juliesevens.com.

Nikki R. Leigh is a queer, forever-90s-kid wallowing in all things horror. When not writing horror fiction and poetry, she can be found creating custom horror-inspired toys, making comics, and hunting vintage paperbacks. She reads her stories to her partner and her cat, one of which gets scared very easily.

Instagram: @spinetinglers; Twitter: @fivexxfive
Website: spinetinglershorror.com
Email: spinetinglersmedia@gmail.com

Marilyn Cavicchia lives in Chicago and is an editor at the American Bar Association as well as a freelance grant writer. Other publications in which her work has recently appeared or is forthcoming include: *The Parliament*, *Hags on Fire*, and *Bureau of Complaint*. Follow her on Twitter @MarilynCavi.

Sarah Budd is a horror writer from London. She has always been fascinated by anything out of the ordinary. Her work has appeared in over twenty magazines and anthologies including *Slash-Her*, NoSleep Podcast, *Diabolica Britannica*, Tales to Terrify, *Aphotic Realm, Sanitarium Magazine, Dark Fire Fiction, Mystic Blue Review, Siren's Call Publications, Deadman's Tome, Innersins, Aphelion, Bewildering Stories*, and *Blood Moon Rising Magazine*. Follow her on Twitter @SjbuddJ, or visit her website: www.sjbudd.co.uk.

Patrick Barb is an author of weird, dark, and horrifying tales, currently living (and trying not to freeze to death) in Saint Paul, Minnesota. He is the author of the dark urban fantasy novella *Gargantuana's Ghost* (forthcoming from Grey Matter Press, Fall 2022), and his short stories appear in a variety of publications, including *Nightscript VIII* (forthcoming), *Diabolical Plots*, and *Boneyard Soup Magazine*. In addition, he is an Active Member of the Horror Writers Association and a Full Member of the Science Fiction and Fantasy Writers Association. For more of his work, visit patrickbarb.com or follow him on Twitter: @pbarb.

Nicholas Alexander Hayes is the author of *Bliss* (Alien Buddha Press, 2022), *Ante-Animots: Idioms and Tales* (BlazeVOX, 2019) and *Amorphous Organics* (SurVision, 2019). He has published essays on '60s gay pulp fiction, vintage beer advertisements, and masculinity on Tumblr.

Ben Walker is a writer and reviewer from the UK, and the editor-owner of Sliced Up Press. His reviews can be found on Kendall Reviews and Ginger Nuts of Horror, as well as his booktube channel, *BLURB*. He can be easily distracted on Twitter @BensNotWriting.

Ann Wuehler has published four novels, *Oregon Gothic, House on Clark Boulevard, Aftermath: Boise, Idaho*, and *The Remarkable Women of Brokenheart Lane*. A short story "Man and Mouse" appeared in the April 2020 issue of *Sun magazine*. Her play, *Bluegrass of God*, was in *Santa Ana River Review*. Her short story "Jimmy's Jar Collection" appeared in the *Ghastling's 13*, and her "The Little Visitors" was in the *Ghastling's 10*. She has five stories placed with Whistle Pig: "Maybelle", "Bunny Slipper", "Pearlie at the Gates of Dawn", "Greenhorn", and "Elbow and Bean". "City Full of Rain" debuted in *Litmag*. "Gladys", a short story, appeared in *Agony Opera*. The short story, the "Elephant Girl", was in the September 2021's the *Bosphorus Review*. "Pig Bait" has been included in *Gore*, an anthology by Poe Boy Publishing, back in October 2021. "The Witch of the Highway", a short story, appeared in the *World of Myth* in October 2021 as well. "Blood and Bread" will appear in Hellbound Books' *Toilet Zone 3, the Royal Flush*, due out in 2022. "Lilith's Arm" was accepted by Bag of Bones to be included in their 2022 *Annus Horribilis* Anthology. "The Salty Monkey Mystery", a short story, will also be published for a charity anthology by Brigids Gate Press.

About the Editors

S.D. Vassallo is a co-founder and editor for Brigids Gate Press, LLC. He's also a writer who loves horror, fantasy, science fiction and crime fiction. He was born and raised in New Orleans, but currently lives in the Midwest with his wife, son, and two black cats who refuse to admit that coyotes exist. When not reading, writing or editing, he can be found gazing at the endless skies of the wide-open prairie. He often spends the night outdoors when the full moon is in sway.

Elle Turpitt is a writer, reviewer, and editor living in Cardiff, Wales. Her short fiction has appeared online, in various anthologies including *Were-Tales* and *The Dead Inside*, and on The NoSleep Podcast. She is co-editor of the anthology *A Woman Built By Man* and co-runs the website Divination Hollow Reviews. Her website is elleturpitt.com and she can be found on Twitter and Instagram @elleturpitt.

ABOUT THE ILLUSTRATOR

Ellen Avigliano is an artist and illustrator based in New Jersey. She is a disabled creator with multiple auto-immune conditions supporting myself with my artwork and creativity. She likes dogs, houseplants, and drinking coffee. She reads a LOT of books. She believes in challenging societal norms, equality and justice for all, and smashing the patriarchy.

She prefers not to "paint myself into a corner" when it comes to media, genre, or style—instead her studio practice has one continual focus across the entire body of work: color! Instead of following the "Academia Mindset" of product-over-process, her creativity focuses heavily on the exploratory process of "making things." Her process is about exploring the endless possibilities of a creative practice, and embracing the wild ride from initial imaginative vision to finished work of art. The freedom She has found in purely experimenting with different media and focusing on the organic nature of creating brings her unparalleled joy!

CONTENT WARNINGS

Find a Friend to Eat Your Pain: domestic violence (off-page).

No Fixed Abode: addiction.

More from Brigids Gate Press

Visit our website at: www.brigidsgatepress.com

Available on Amazon

A terrifying pandemic sweeps the world, rendering its victims completely immobile but leaving them conscious with their minds intact. The victims are helpless against the environment, completely at the mercy of wild animals, weather, out of control fires, and other dangers. There's no hope for those safe in their homes either, as they slowly starve to death, unable to feed themselves or drink

Dr. Alex Griffiths leads a team racing against time to find a cure before it's too late. Will he succeed?

Available wherever books are sold

Decades after his grandfather was buried alive in a Californian gold mine, Dr. Nick Jones teams up with an adventure travel influencer to venture underground and film a documentary, telling the story of what really happened.

What should be a dream come true soon becomes a nightmare as someone or something stirs…BELOW.

Available wherever books are sold

A Quaint and Curious Volume of Gothic Tales; 23 stories of madness, pain, ghosts, curses, unspoken secrets, greed, murder, and one of the creepiest collections of dolls ever. Ranging from traditional gothic themes to more modern tropes, this anthology is sure to please the reader…and send a cold shiver or two down their spine.

So, come on in; enter the parlor, find a place by the fire, and experience the beautiful, dark, and occasionally heartbreaking stories told by the authors. The editor, Alex Woodroe, has passionately and carefully curated a powerful volume of stories, written by an amazing and diverse group of contemporary women writers.

Coming in August 2022

On the run from a life of prostitution and poverty, exotic dancer Cece Dulac agrees to become the main attraction at an erotic séance hosted by an enigmatic mesmerist, Monsieur Rossignol. As the séance descends into depravity, Cece falls prey to Rossignol's hypnotic power and becomes possessed by a malevolent spirit.

George Dashwood, an aspiring artist, witnesses the séance and fears for Cece. He seeks her out and she seduces him, but she is no longer herself. The spirit controlling her forces her to commit increasingly depraved acts. When the spirit's desire for revenge escalates to murder, George and Cece must find a way to break Rossignol's spell before Cece's soul is condemned forever.

Marionette is an erotic horror novella inspired by traditional folk tales and set in fin de siècle Paris.

Coming September 2022

During the Spring Equinox underneath London, four people enter the caves, but only one will survive. Each trespasser must battle their own demons before facing the White Lady who rises each year to feed on human flesh.

www.ingramcontent.com/pod-product-compliance
Lightning Source LLC
Chambersburg PA
CBHW031028190726
48286CB00003BA/1066